Praise for Tom I

The Kid &

"*Everyone should have the desire to never stop growing and learning. This book,* Mentor: The Kid & The CEO, *reminds us that mentors are a great way to achieve success in your physical, mental, spiritual, financial and social areas of your life. A quick read, this book is a must at all ages.*"

— Dr. Gary Smalley, Author of
Change Your Heart, Change Your Life

"*Thank you! Couldn't be more timely!*"
— Steve Forbes, President & CEO, Forbes Magazine

"*There's much to learn in life and I am grateful that people like Tom Pace are willing to teach us. This is a compelling story and a powerful message.*"
— Mick Cornett, Mayor, Oklahoma City

"*I have enjoyed your new book,* Mentor: The Kid & The CEO. *It is very inspirational and will challenge readers to get involved in the lives of others to make a difference. Thank you for sharing your wonderful insight and encouragement.*"
— Mary Fallin, Member of United States Congress
Fifth District, Oklahoma

"Compelling from the very first page. Tom mentors all of us with his steps to success."
~ Ron Moore, CEO, Dale Carnegie of Oklahoma

"It compelled me to get back into the learning process. Quite frankly, I had been so busy living and working, that I had not been spending time growing. Thanks for the encouragement to grow and help others."
~ Rod N. Baker, CEO,
Baker First Commercial Real Estate

"This book is amazing! I read it and now I'm reading it again with my wife. Thank you for making such wonderful principles so easy to read about and learn."
~ Mike Foster, Consultant

"Thanks again for the book! It was an amazing read and I'm going to buy more. Keep up the great work!"
~ Tim Strange, CCIM, SIOR,
Managing Director, Sperry Van Ness

"Mentor: The Kid & The CEO is just what my nephew needed. It motivated him to get into a program, get a positive mentor and he is making the changes necessary to become successful. As a college professor I am anxious to refer the book to students and use the material in the

classroom. *Mentoring may be the most important component missing in higher education today!"*

~ J. David Chapman,
University of Central Oklahoma, and CEO of Realty1

"I just finished reading the book Mentor: The Kid & the CEO. It was an amazing, inspiring, easy-to-read book that I could hardly put down! We would like to distribute a book to each of our members and guests during our Annual Banquet. This is definitely a "pay it forward" book that should be passed around! Whether a member of the Fredericksburg Volunteer Rescue Squad, or another volunteer agency, civic club, church, school, etc. this book is sure to "JUMP START" everyone's "MENTOR BATTERIES!"

~ Barbara Branham, Life Member,
Fredericksburg Volunteer Rescue Squad, Inc.

"Here is a book that makes you think about life. It reminds you that your destiny is in your own hands. I truly enjoyed reading it and have ordered 10 more copies to give to friends."

~ Amir Farzaneh, Immigration Attorney, Hall Estill

"Thanks for the book! I finished it waiting to go home from KC to OKC. The book spurred lots of thoughts. I feel invigorated, determined, thoughts of serving more in

*this life. I will be challenging my son to read this book
and telling my friends about it"*
— Tom Garret, Regional Sales Manager,
Walgreens Home Care

"Thank you so much for writing Mentor: The Kid and
The CEO. *The recommended reading list in the back of
your book is inspiring. I immediately made a copy and
started tracking the books I have completed. Your list is
an excellent starting point for anyone who wishes to
achieve true significance."*
— Brett Windsor, Business Express Banking

*"We send out a monthly pack to members of our group
that contains a book and audios. The material we use is
geared toward business building, motivation, inspiration, mentoring, etc. We have 750 members in the group.
This book would be perfect to distribute to them."*
— Janine Burch

*"...an easy read with lots of value. It gave me inspiration and
motivation to tackle all areas of my life; not only as a business woman and single mom, but in my personal life as
well. My teenage daughter also read the book and was inspired to take up cross country running. This book is a must
read for all, regardless of what season of life you are in!"*
— Pam Fleharty, Business Professional

"I started reading your book. I hardly know what to say! I absolutely love it! The message is clear and compelling. This book is speaking to me on many different levels. I would like to be like Malcolm. But in many ways, I am so much like Tony. I think this book is going to make a big difference. I want to distribute them in quantity."
~ Robin Khoury, Writer, Publisher

"This book caused me to re-evaluate how I was living many aspects of my life. It gave me the inspiration I needed to take action, improving those areas and myself in general. It is a very quick and easy to read book with a story line that makes it hard to put down. I am grateful that I've had the opportunity to read it."
~ Dustin Wiese, Manager

"After reading this book, I understand that having a mentor in my life is the most important decision I can make for my future." ~ Chase Turner, Student

"This book delivers a message that is simple but not often understood: The journey in pursuit of personal development is its own reward ~ pay it forward and it pays you back. Everyone can find a part of themselves in the characters of this story and it came along at just the right time for me." ~ Jeff Beller, Musician

MENTOR
THE KID
&
THE
CEO

MENTOR
THE KID
&
THE
CEO

A SIMPLE STORY OF ACHIEVING SIGNIFICANCE

TOM PACE with Walter Jenkins

SECOND EDITION

Learn. Teach. Do.

MENTOR·HOPE

MENTORHOPE PUBLISHING
Edmond, Oklahoma

MENTOR: The Kid and The CEO;
A Simple Story of Achieving Significance
by Tom Pace with Walter Jenkins
2nd Edition

Published by MentorHope Publishing,
an imprint of Gaines Taylor Banks Publishing
13915 N. Harvey Ave., Edmond, OK 73013
Telephone: 1-405-752-0940

This book is available in volume for qualifying organizations. Please contact
the publisher to inquire.

For more information about this book or mentoring, please visit
www.mentorhope.com

Cover and interior design by Pneuma Books, LLC
www.pneumabooks.com

Publisher's Cataloging-In-Publication Data
(Prepared by The Donohue Group, Inc.)

Pace, Thomas Alan.
    Mentor : the kid & the CEO / Tom Pace, with Walter Jenkins.

        p. ; cm.

    "A simple story of [overcoming challenges and] achieving significance."
    Includes bibliographical references.
    ISBN: 978-0-9793962-4-3 (second edition hardcover)
    ISBN: 978-0-9793962-7-4 (first edition hardcover)
    ISBN: 978-0-9793962-3-6 (second edition resale pbk.)
    ISBN: 978-0-9793962-2-9 (second edition non-resale gift pbk.)
    ISBN: 978-0-9793962-6-7 (first edition pbk.)

1. Mentoring—Fiction. 2. Success—Fiction. 3. Self-realization—Fiction.
4. Chief executive officers—Fiction. 5. Prisoners—Fiction. I. Jenkins, Walter.
II. Title. III. Title: Mentor : the kid and the CEO

PS3616.A24 M46 2007
813/.6   2007924814

Printed in the United States of America

20 19 18 17 16 15 14 13 12 11   01 02 03 04 05 06 07 08 09 10

www.MentorHope.com

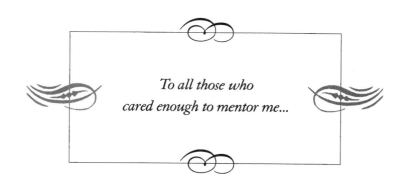

To all those who
cared enough to mentor me...

CONTENTS

1

CAUGHT

I can't believe I'm in here again. I promised myself I would never be back.

I fell back into the lower bunk, my head in my hands. The other inmates were watching TV at the end of the unit so I knew I wouldn't be disturbed. I could afford a few moments to myself.

It's probably not the same cell as last time, but it's identical. The big metal gray door, the tiny window, the two "roommates." Just like last time. The cells are made for two, but they never just put two in them, do they? I hate this place. It stinks

Finish what you start.

worse than the high school locker room after football practice. And the air never moves. Everyone in here stinks. I stink.

The negative thoughts would not stop swirling around in my head. I looked down at my county-issued orange jumpsuit, white socks, and foam sandals. "It's not even my fault," I said out loud to the empty cell.

I can't believe I got arrested again, and for something so stupid, I thought.

It started as a way for me to have a good time. It was just beer, no big deal. Jeff, my best friend, and I were shooting the breeze on Jeff's front porch. He lives two blocks from my house.

"Cold beer sure would be good right now," Jeff said.

"Sure would," I agreed. I knew that drinking on a suspended sentence was against the rules, but who would find out? Nobody would even care. "Got any cash?"

"Nope. Don't need it." Jeff winked at me, reached in his pocket for the keys to his pickup, and motioned for me to follow. I knew what he wanted to do. Neither of us spoke as he drove the truck to the convenience store. We left it running and both got out.

We walked in and smiled at the clerk. He looked at us and returned to counting cartons of cigarettes. I wasn't wor-

Pick up trash.

ried about him. He was just some fool working for a few bucks an hour. He probably wouldn't even try to stop us.

We went to the back corner of the store. Jeff and I both grabbed a twelve-pack of beer and headed toward the counter. The clerk stopped counting, turned toward the register, and had just enough time to see us laugh and run to the truck. The clerk was on the phone by the time I closed the passenger door.

Jeff backed the truck away. I tore open the box of beer and grabbed a single can. We both laughed like crazy because we got away with it. Jeff drove the truck out of the parking lot, turned right, and headed south. He waited until he'd made the turn to pull the light switch on so that the license plate would not be illuminated. Just three more turns and we'd be home free — well on the way to a great night.

Not one second after the lights came on, the truck died. That's when we stopped laughing. I looked at Jeff in amazement. How could he plan a stunt like this without enough gas in his truck? I was terrified. The store was less than a block away.

It must have been a slow night for the cops. A police cruiser pulled up behind us with its overhead lights on. And that was it. All I could do was cup my head in my

Have integrity.

hands and shake it in disbelief. My chest tightened, my heart beat faster, and my mind raced, wondering, *How will I tell Mom? How long am I going to be locked up? What kind of life will I have now that I've been arrested again?*

It's not even my fault. If that idiot *had just put some gas in the truck, neither one of us would have been caught. My life sucks.*

None of that mattered now. Nothing mattered.

Have values.

2

BACK IN JAIL

The last time I was in the Oklahoma County Jail was six months ago. I wound up with a suspended sentence on a second-degree burglary charge.

My court-appointed lawyer warned me about staying out of trouble. "Don't get a speeding ticket or even a parking ticket. Don't even jaywalk. If you get in any trouble at all, you could do up to seven years in prison. Son, do you understand?"

He asked like he was my dad. I felt like a kid. I didn't need to be treated like a kid. Who did he think he was?

Be a mentor.

He'd never even talked to me before he agreed to plead me on a felony charge. If I'd had the money for a *real* lawyer, I would have never been convicted.

"Sure." What did he expect me to say: Next time, I'll be smarter and not get caught?

I nodded in agreement, and I meant to stay out of trouble, too. I had no desire to ever go back to jail, no desire to ever be searched or fingerprinted again, and no desire to eat bologna sandwiches. But here I sit, arrested for something even stupider than the last time.

The worst part was seeing how disappointed my mom was after I agreed to plead guilty. She's always tried to get me to do the right thing. I'd let her down again. I could see in her eyes how upset she was. I wished I had never been caught.

Mom wore her Sunday dress. She was embarrassed to take the day off from work to come to court to see her oldest son plead guilty to a felony. She had to pass through a metal detector. The detector went off and she was searched. They even treated *her* like a criminal. I can't believe I put her through all that — that was the last thing I'd wanted.

She did her best to raise us right, and now I'm in jail

Stay committed.

again. It's not her fault, but it's not mine either. Who forgets to put gas in the getaway car? Despite all my promises and good intentions I was back in jail again — and it wasn't even my fault.

Listen well.

3

90 DAYS TO WAIT

It's been seven days and they're just now taking me to see the judge. All this fuss over some stupid beer. Don't they have any real criminals to catch?

When I woke up, the guard told me I had to go to court. I hoped that meant someone had realized how stupid it was that I was in jail for a twelve-pack of beer. I mean, they could let a guy go for something as stupid as that, right? I thought they might let me out, so I was more than happy to head to the courtroom while I was still half asleep.

Don't take things personally.

The judge looked at all of us prisoners chained together. "Will the defendant please approach the bench?"

Some guard grabbed me by the shoulder. I walked over to the judge, my hands cuffed in front of me.

"Sir, do you know why you are here?" came a voice from behind the bench. All I could see was a black robe and a pair of glasses.

"Yes, ma'am. My friend and I stole some beer and we got caught." My attorney had shown me some paperwork before the judge arrived. No, I don't really understand all the fuss over some beer, but does it matter? Why did she even ask me? Was she really going to listen to anything I had to say?

"According to what I have here, six months ago you came before this court and pled guilty to a charge of burglary in the second degree. At that time you agreed to a suspended sentence, which meant if you lived by certain terms and conditions, instead of going to prison for seven years, you could stay out. Is that correct?"

"Yes, Your Honor." I didn't like where this conversation was heading. I started having trouble breathing. Where is the part about me going home?

"Yet here we are again, and you have now been

Give away a book.

charged with..." the judge ruffled through some papers on her desk and pulled two sheets out "...stealing beer. You violated the agreement we made six months ago." She shook her head.

"How old are you, sir?"

"Nineteen."

"Nineteen," she said, like I should get some kind of prize for living that long. The judge took the reading glasses off her nose and threw them on her desk like she was really pissed. What a staged presentation. I bet she gives the same show for everybody who comes into her courtroom. She ought to charge admission. "You must really be in a hurry to get to prison."

All my blood rushed to my face. My stomach turned sour. My knees started to knock. Only my pride kept me from falling down.

The judge continued, "Sir, the district attorney has filed paperwork to revoke your suspended sentence. What they are asking me to do is to send you to prison for seven years."

The court was silent.

They're going to send me to prison over some stolen beer?

Open doors for people.

Then the judge said, "And, quite frankly, I am inclined to agree."

Prison? Because of twelve beers? I wanted to say: You're crazy. It's twelve cans of beer! But I kept my mouth shut and tried to look cool. My heart was pounding so fast it felt like it was about to explode. Was I mad or scared? It was hard to tell.

"However, here is what we are going to do. I am going to pass this matter on my docket for ninety days. That means three months from now you will come back before me and I will determine if you will go to prison, and, if so, for how long. During these ninety days, you will stay in jail. And for ninety days, you need to think long and hard as to why I should not send you to prison. Don't think for one second that I won't. All it takes is for me to sign the paperwork. Do I make myself clear?"

My mind raced to keep up. The last thing I'd heard was "ninety days." Each time the judge said those words they became louder and louder, blocking everything else out.

The court-appointed attorney nudged me. At least he was useful for that. He hadn't done anything else for me. What a loser. I took a breath for what felt like the first time since I'd entered the courtroom. I went over the judge's

Help others.

words in my mind and finally managed to say, "Yes, Your Honor."

"Good. You are dismissed."

Another set of hands grabbed me from behind, took me back to the other defendants, and shackled me at the end of the line.

Four hours since I left the courtroom and I still want to throw up. My life is over, I thought. I have a felony conviction. I couldn't stay out of jail and I'm probably going to prison. It's not even my fault.

Only ninety days to go.

Ask questions.

4

"GROUP"

I was sitting in my bunk wondering what, if anything, my future held when the guard yelled out, "Anyone want to go to group?" My cellmates left and I listened to their feet shuffle down the hallway. I wasn't going anywhere. I was happy to see them go. At least I could be alone for a while and have some privacy. Thoughts were swirling in my head and I didn't want to do anything. What was the point? What could I do that would make my life better? Had I known what was happening, I would have run to the meeting.

Encourage others.

I stared at the wall until I heard laughter coming from the hallway. It was my cellmates returning from group. I had no idea how much time had passed since they'd left. One of my cellmates came in, sat down on his bed, and began reading a book.

All I could do was think about my life that would never change. *I don't know if I will ever live outside a jail again. I can't get a break.*

Only eighty-three days to go. I had not seen anything other than the inside of my cell, inmates, and guards since my court date. Occasionally a new inmate would arrive and break up the boredom, but for the most part the days and nights melted together.

There was one inmate I couldn't help but notice. Everyone did. He was well over six feet tall and must have weighed 240 pounds. He was bald. But most important, the guy was solid muscle.

Another inmate filled me in.

"His name is Charles and he gets what he wants. Even in here. Don't mess with him. If he asks for it, give it. He could break somebody like you in half. He's doing life on

Move someone for free.

a murder charge. He's here on a different case waiting to be transferred to prison."

He was right. There was no way I could stop Charles from taking anything he wanted. And I mean anything.

I'd always been told I was a nice looking kid. Five feet ten and 170 pounds. People always said I had a boyish face. Whatever.

Sometimes being cute isn't all that great, I thought. *I'm a virgin, at least in some ways, and I want to stay that way. Charles isn't my type, and I hope I'm not his.* I didn't want to be his.

After dinner, which I'm pretty sure was actually Gainesburgers with rice and warm milk, the guard called out for group.

"Who wants to go?"

The prisoner above me got out of his bunk and put on his slippers.

"What's group?" I asked.

"Oh, we just talk about stuff."

"Like what?"

"Work, freedom, books, traveling, God. That kind of stuff."

I didn't know much about any of that, but I wanted out

Pick up trash.

of the cell. I had been in the same place with the same people breathing the same air for seven days. I put on my sandals, followed the other inmates, and headed for the end of the unit, where the tables were. Going to that first meeting was a great decision.

I found an empty table and sat down. Two other guys eventually sat down with me and said hello.

At the front of the room was a guy who was definitely an outsider — the only person that I had seen in a week who wasn't wearing a uniform. His silver hair was combed back and his skin was slightly tanned. He wore a T-shirt, shorts, and sandals. Leather sandals — not the cheap foam kind like they were making me wear. The leather band of his watch matched his brown shoes.

Lucky guy. I envied anyone who could come and go as he pleased. Must be nice to be able to walk out of this lousy stinkhole.

"All right guys, time to get started." The outsider spoke loudly and clearly. The conversation at the other tables came to a complete stop, as if the other prisoners knew something valuable was going to happen and they did not want to miss it. Inmates did not get that quiet, even for the guards.

Be cheerful.

"Thank you all very much for coming, and thank you for giving me the opportunity to speak to you tonight. For those of you who don't know, my name is Malcolm and I'd like to...."

I didn't hear another word that night. Instead, I let my mind wander and I thought about a few questions. *Why would a person give up his time to come talk to a bunch of people in jail? What does this guy think he can teach me? Does he just come down here every so often to make himself feel better? Probably won't see him again.*

After the meeting, everyone was smiling and slapping each other on the back. For a moment, it didn't feel like jail. Everybody was friendly. Malcolm, or whatever his name was, had brought some books with him, and he handed them out to anyone who wanted one. There's lots of time to read in jail.

The sound of inmates getting up from their seats at the end of the meeting pulled me back to reality. The outsider was shaking hands. He gave someone a little blue book.

I headed down the dingy, fluorescent-lit hall. I'd left without taking a book. As I walked back to my cell I could still hear the laughter bouncing off the concrete walls, and I tried to remember the last time I had laughed.

Be a giver.

When I got back to my cell, I couldn't even remember what the outsider had talked about. I couldn't recall one word. But I did remember the hope those guys seemed to have.

One of my cellmates finally made it back in. He was holding a book. He jumped into his bunk, moved his pillow, and began reading.

Be kind.

5

A BLUE BOOK

It had been fourteen days since I'd been in front of the judge. Only seventy-six more to go. Everything had melted together into one giant heap of orange jumpsuits, sweat, and bologna sandwiches.

I needed to use the restroom and went to the common toilet at the back of the cell. *This sucks.* That was about all I could think about while I relieved myself in front of two cellmates. I usually asked my cellmates to leave so I could have some privacy. I wondered if I would ever again pee without an audience.

Save 10 percent.

Before I could finish, I heard the guard make his Monday call. "Time for group. Who wants to go?" For a moment I had privacy to finish my business as my cellmates shuffled to the meeting.

I decided to go to group too. Why not take advantage of the one-hour interruption to my boredom? I couldn't imagine that one day these meetings would become so important to me.

I found an empty table and sat down. I liked to be the first one to sit down at a table because I didn't have to make eye contact or ask anyone for permission. Other prisoners milled about; eventually everyone found a seat.

A voice boomed from behind me. "Thank you all very much for coming, and I especially thank you for giving me the opportunity to speak with you tonight."

My mind drifted away. The meeting ended sometime later. I let some of the other inmates head down the hall. I saw Malcolm out of the corner of my eye heading toward me. What did this goody-two-shoes want with me?

"Hello. My name is Malcolm. I don't believe I've had the chance to meet you yet," said Malcolm, extending his hand toward me.

Visit someone in the hospital.

I put out my right hand and felt Malcolm's hand close around it. He asked me my name and how old I was.

"I'm Tony. I'm nineteen."

"Listen Tony, I know it's boring in here, with nothing to stare at but the walls. I want to give you a book that will make a difference in your life."

"Sure." What else could I say? It's boring in jail. There's not a whole lot going on in here. Did he figure that out all by himself? What a genius.

I've never been a big fan of reading. It usually puts me to sleep. It's hard for me to remember what I've read. Some teachers said I might be dyslexic; others said I probably have attention deficit disorder.

"If you get a chance, read this book, will you?"

"Okay." I would have said anything to get this guy off my back. What difference does it make? I wasn't going to see him again, anyway.

I took the book and headed back to my cell. *Whatever*, I thought. *Like I'm going to waste my time reading.* Then I noticed the title: *The Greatest Miracle in the World.* Miracle? *Yeah, right.*

I sat on my bunk, slipped off my worn out foam slippers,

Visit someone in treatment.

and put them under my bed. I put the book on top of them and went to sleep.

The following morning I tossed the book on my bunk and put on my sandals. The book landed cover up and stayed there for the rest of the day.

That afternoon, I saw one of the other guys looking at the book. It was one of the inmates who went to group on Monday nights.

"Is that your book?" he asked, pointing to my bunk.

"Uh... I guess. Some do-gooder gave it to me."

"Malcolm?"

"Yeah. That's his name."

"Have you read it yet?"

"No." What was this? Twenty Questions? I might as well have been back in court, being cross-examined.

"Do yourself a favor. Read it. I don't know how to explain it, but it's a pretty cool book. And that guy, Malcolm, I know somebody he helped. Since he met Malcolm, he hasn't been back in this lousy place. And Malcolm helped him start his own business."

"Okay. I'll give it a shot." Will he leave me alone now? I told him what he wanted to hear.

Believe in yourself.

The book sat, unopened, for the next three days. Like I said, I'm not a big fan of reading.

Have a dream list.

6

CHARLES

On Saturday, just after lunch, I was alone in my cell. I had my back to the open door when I felt the urge to turn around. Standing there, in the doorway, was my worst nightmare. It was Charles.

I froze. The hair on the back of my neck stood up, and my heart began to pound. About the last thing I wanted was to be alone in the cell with him. All the air in the room seemed to disappear as my chest tightened. Charles took one step into the cell. His eyes were scanning side to side,

Use a to-do list.

up and down. His jaw was clenched tight; muscles bulged from the side of his head.

I had no idea what to do. Charles stood between me and the door. The wrong move would be dangerous. Any move would probably be dangerous. Even if nobody had ever told me not to mess with Charles, one look at him would have told me not to. I imagined Charles picking me up and breaking me in half.

What does he want? What can I give him? There's nothing in this cell...but me, I thought. *This is really uncool. How can I get out of this?*

Charles looked around and noticed the book on my bunk. "Where'd ya get that?"

The question hit me like an explosion. I felt as though I'd jumped out of my skin. My eyes followed Charles's arm down to his outstretched finger. It was pointing to my bunk. "Where'd you get that book?" he repeated.

"Malcolm gave it to me."

Charles looked at the book and then at me. Just for a second, his jaw relaxed and the narrow slits that covered his eyes opened.

"Sit down."

Don't worry.

This request was not open to negotiation. It was an order. I obeyed immediately, moving to the bunk furthest from my visitor. I knew enough to keep my mouth shut.

"I've been in and out of this place for most of my life. I just got another case, and soon I'll be transferred back to state. I don't know the last time I spent a full month without being cuffed.

"That guy, Malcolm, I've seen him in here every Monday that I've been in. And that's a bunch of Mondays. Don't think he's ever missed one. He's probably the only guy in this whole place who cares one bit about me or you or anybody else.

"I've seen a lot of people come and go through these walls. Most of 'em did their time like you, walking around like a dead man. But then there's some that came through here and listened to what Malcolm said. They're on the outside now, living good lives. I know.

"So what you need to do is to listen to him, read what he tells you to read, do what he tells you to do. Get outta here and make something of yourself. Don't wind up an old criminal like me."

With that, Charles turned around and left. Gone as quickly as he had come.

Visit someone in jail.

When Charles was completely out of sight, I forced myself to take a deep breath. Another deep breath. Another. I found the courage to stand but had to grab onto the top bunk to keep from falling.

What is it with this book? It just saved me from Charles, and I haven't even opened the front cover yet. Maybe it really is a miracle book. Maybe I'll go ahead and find out what it says on the inside.

Ideas. Action. Commitment.

7

A MIRACLE

"Who wants to go to group?" It was the one phrase I could count on to break up the boredom of the week. I picked up my book (there was no way I was going to let Charles see me going to group without it) and headed down the hallway.

I actually listened in group this week. No daydreams this time. Probably the first smart thing I had done in years.

At the end of the session Malcolm approached me. "Hey, Tony," he said, putting out his hand.

I was surprised that Malcolm remembered my name. It

Visit someone in a homeless shelter.

felt uncomfortable to be called by my first name in this place. Not only that, but he had a big smile on his face. That, too, seemed out of place here.

"Did you read the book yet?" Malcolm noticed it in my hand.

It took me a second to answer. I thought about lying, but then he could have asked me about the book. I hadn't read it, and Malcolm deserved respect, so I told him the truth. "I won't lie to you. No, I haven't read it." I was worried about the wrong person finding out that I had lied to Malcolm. But something also told me that he had knowledge to offer. Something about Malcolm caused people to say such good things about him, and I did not want to miss out on that.

Malcolm smiled and said, "Well, kid, at least you're honest."

I didn't like being called a kid, but I was only nineteen. Maybe this old man could teach me something.

"Tony, I know that people see me come in here and wonder what I'm doing, But ask around, I really want to help you. I really *do* help people.

"People need to read so that they can learn from history and from famous people. If you read you can learn from

Buy someone dinner.

people who want to share their experience so that you can have a better quality of life. If you read, you will never be alone.

"So, when I ask you to do this, I'm not doing it for me but for you. Will you please read that book by next week?"

I looked Malcolm in the eyes. "Yes."

I almost instantly regretted it. Not only was I in jail; now I had homework.

The book sat on my bunk for two days. *Why didn't I just say no?* I was frustrated at the thought I had not been man enough to tell Malcolm I was not interested in reading, much less some stupid book about miracles.

Miracles? Yeah, right. Like anything like that would happen to someone like me. Then I recalled how the book had saved me from Charles.

I looked out of my cell and saw Charles playing cards at the center of the unit. That jarred me back to the moment. That and a gnawing feeling that I did not want to break the promise I had made to Malcolm.

I reluctantly began reading that afternoon At first, my only desire was to finish the book so that I could tell Malcolm I had read it. I also thought about skipping group

Exercise.

from now on and sending the book back with one of my cellmates. I was pretty sure that Charles would find out about that though.

But by the time I got to page three, I became curious about the book and what it was talking about. Some parts of it seemed to be talking directly to me. By Sunday night I had finished it, and my mind was busy thinking over what I had read.

I had hope for the first time in years that I meant something and that I had a bright future. Reading that book made me realize that if I made better choices and educated myself, I could do things I had not dreamed of before.

For the first time, I really looked forward to going to group. I felt great just because I'd read the book ~ the first book I'd ever read cover to cover. Now that really was *the greatest miracle in the world*!

"Time for group. Any takers?" That was the announcement that I had been waiting for. I let a few other prisoners head down the hall before me, so that I would not seem too anxious. Of course, I remembered to bring my book with me.

Take vitamins.

I found a seat near the front so that I could talk to Malcolm at the end of the meeting. This time I really listened.

Malcolm began with his usual greeting. I noticed how he looked around the room as he talked. Actually, he didn't look around the room, but from person to person, being sure to make eye contact with each one. He seemed to be speaking to each individual person.

It was cool how Malcolm actually listened to people when they had a question. He didn't just try to get them to shut up.

I thought about all that I had heard about Malcolm. He did show up every week. And he treated us with respect, even though we were wearing orange jail uniforms.

I wanted to ask Malcolm a few questions; but by the time we were face to face, I didn't have the nerve. I decided to just tell him I had read the book and leave.

"Hello, Tony." Once again the eyes and the handshake. "Did you read the book?"

"Yes, sir. Sure did." I was proud that I had completed the book. I had read it cover to cover. It felt great to finish something I started.

"So, what did you think?"

Finish what you start.

"Are you some kind of Simon Potter yourself?" I asked. We both laughed.

"Do you have any questions?"

I didn't know what to say. The wrong answer here and I might end up with more homework. But I did have questions, not just about the book but about Malcolm, too.

"Well..." was all I could get out.

"Have a seat."

Malcolm knew I had questions, but he started talking, which was good, because I didn't know what to say. I'll never forget what he told me.

"Tony, I've been doing this a long time. I've been handing out books for years. How many people do you think read the books that I hand out? There are many books written, but few are read," he said, smiling. "But you took the action and read the book, and you got something out of it. That's great.

"What separates winners from losers is action, and the right kind of action. Reading gives you knowledge, and with that you have the power to do what you want. Most people don't read; but because you read, you have hope."

I listened, but I had no idea where Malcolm was going with this.

Winners take action.

"You might be surprised to hear that I've been in your shoes. I remember when I was first handed that book. I thought it was a joke. I had never in my life read a complete book, from cover to cover. And I didn't want to read that one. But I did. And I had questions, just like almost everybody who's ever read it has questions. And the questions are almost always the same.

"No one ever wants to admit they have questions, but let me give you the answers anyway.

"The answer to your big question is: Yes, Tony, that book is speaking about you and to you. Everything in that book that talks about people being miracles, about them having a purpose in life, about them being able to change and get out of the messes they have created, that was written for you and about you."

I sat in stunned silence. Parts of the book had jumped off the page. Sentences whispered they were just for me, with meanings that no one else could understand. How could Malcolm know this?

I watched Malcolm speak. He spoke enthusiastically. I could tell he truly believed what he was saying. It sounds corny, but I started feeling enthusiastic myself, even here in jail.

Share hope.

"That was what you wanted to know, right?"

"Yes." I could barely get the words out. "I just wanted to know if that stuff was really true."

"It is. Do you want to learn more?"

"Yes."

"Good. Here's what I want you to do. Re-read that book this week. Next week, we will go over it together. Will you do that for me?"

"Yes." For a second, I couldn't believe I said it. More homework. This time, I decided it was worth it.

And with that, Malcolm said, "Now, it's time for me to go, so I will see you at the next meeting."

We stood up, shook hands, and I watched Malcolm leave the room.

Dream big.

8

THE CEO

I started reading the next morning. For the second night in a row I slept better than I had in a long time. I was eager to start applying what Malcolm was teaching me.

By Friday, I had read the book a second time. It was so powerful I could barely put it down. I started folding down corners on the pages that I had questions about. I wanted to talk to Malcolm about them.

By Monday, I'd read each of these pages for a third time. That evening I hardly waited for the guard to finish his

Winners plan.

announcement before I started down the hallway, book in hand. I found a seat in front and got Malcolm's attention.

"Malcolm, I re-read the book, just like you asked."

"Great. We'll talk after group."

There was another outsider with Malcolm. He was slender, and, like Malcolm, was wearing jeans and a T-shirt. The outsider must have been about ten years older than I was. Probably about twenty-eight or so. He looked like the kind of guy that had been locked up before, but there was something different about him. His face was relaxed; it wasn't tense like the guys in jail. He stood next to Malcolm and they waited for the seats at the tables to fill up.

The thought flashed through my mind that one day I would be able to come back here with Malcolm. One day I could be the one standing in front of the group as an example to others.

After his greeting, Malcolm introduced the new face. "Guys, this is Gary. He used to be in here just like you. But he worked hard and started doing things differently. Now he's on the outside, making good money. And best of all, he's going to stay out."

Gary smiled, stepped forward, and nodded to the group.

Call a friend.

"Gary will be here after the meeting so that you can speak to him. Or, if you want, you can ask him questions during group. Are you ready to get started?"

Group went along just like it had the last few weeks. Malcolm spoke, people listened, and a few asked questions.

The only thing unusual was one inmate who kept talking. He talked forever. I wondered if he'd ever shut up.

Malcolm's reaction was remarkable to me. He never cut the guy off, never stopped him. He just smiled, listened, and let the man speak. He seemed to really pay attention to the words the guy was saying.

After group Malcolm met a few guys, shook hands, and gave out books. Some books appeared the same as the book Malcolm gave me; some were different. I watched as the guys thinned out. Gary came over to say good-bye to Malcolm when he finished talking to a few of the guys. I was the only one to stay late.

Malcolm and I went through the book together. I showed him the pages I had questions on, and Malcolm explained what everything meant.

I was amazed at everything Malcolm knew. "How do you know all this?"

"I've been doing this a long time. And I've been in your

Planners win.

shoes. Now I read everything I can. I've learned a lot from reading. You can't read too much."

I didn't know what to say so I just kept quiet.

"Look at this jail. You deserve better. You were made for more than this. That's what this book is about."

I couldn't believe that anyone would say something like that to me. No one had ever talked to me like this before. He talked to me like I really was special. This guy gave me hope, and I could feel something inside me start to move.

"You're special, Tony. What I will do is help you to become a winner. And there's nothing different about me. I've had days where I didn't know where my next dime was coming from. But I then started to listen and learn. People taught me a different way of thinking, a better way of being, and I can pass that knowledge on to you. Are you ready?"

"Yes."

"Are you ready to take action if I show you what to do? Because I can *show* you what to do, but I can't do it for you."

"What can I do in here?" The gray cinder block walls and stale air made any change seem impossible.

"You don't know it yet, but you were in prison long before the police ever put handcuffs on you. Now the prison

Learn from other people.

I'm talking about is not a building with bars or razor wire fencing, but it's still the most powerful jail on earth.

"The prison I'm talking about is right up here." Malcolm tapped his right index finger against his temple. "Your mind.

"What you can do in here is remember that you are special and that your life has meaning. You can start to do things differently. You can start to tear down the prison in your mind."

I didn't really understand Malcolm, but something inside me told me to believe him. Even Charles, the most feared man in the jail, respected him. I decided right there to trust Malcolm.

"A prison in my mind? What do you mean?" I asked.

"Most people have never been taught to think about how many great things they can do. I learned this one simple truth and it made a huge difference in my life. I will teach you what I've learned."

So Malcolm spoke and I listened for a long time. Listening to him felt a little like eating a big meal when you're starving, and I felt the words go right to my soul.

After a while, Malcolm asked, "Tony, do you know what a mentor is?"

Do good.

I didn't.

"A mentor is like a teacher, but more. A mentor helps someone develop their life. There are five important parts of your life: physical, mental, spiritual, financial, and social. I can help you grow in these areas. Would you like me to mentor you?"

"Yes."

Malcolm said, "There's something else I want you to do. Have you ever heard of a dream list?"

"No."

"A dream list is a list of everything you want out of life. Start writing one this week."

"How do I do that?"

"It's easy. Just think about the things that you want to do. And be specific. You want a car, right?"

"Yeah." Who doesn't?

"Well, I want you to think about what kind of car, what year, what color. Then write that down.

"Then you think about other stuff you want, like a house. Think about places you want to go, like New York City, Florida, South America, wherever. It's your list and there are no wrong answers.

Use good manners.

"Think about people you want to meet, like movie stars, actresses, leaders, or politicians.

"Think about how strong you want to be, how healthy. Think about your friends; about how you get along with your family; how you want to feel about yourself and your spiritual life."

I asked, "Why do I do all that?"

"Because once you put your dreams on paper, I can help you get the things on your list. That's what a mentor does."

Malcolm continued, "And dream big. Don't skimp on your dream list. There may be some things that you want but are afraid to write down. Maybe you think it's stupid for you to want something like that.

"Don't censor your thoughts when you make the list. Any place you want to go, anything you want, or anyone you want to meet, put that on your list. Once we have a list we can start working toward making those things become real."

"Okay," I agreed, having no idea how I would start. I would try. No one had ever spoken to me about dreams. At best, I was a C student — and that was on a good day. I'd never felt like I had the right to ask for anything fancy — things like fancy vacations, cars, and meeting important

Call a relative.

people. Those were just for important people. Not someone like me. My idea of a car was something that started and didn't break down every day. As for trips, I had only been out of the state once. That was a drive down to Dallas. Just a few hours in the car.

Hearing Malcolm talk about these things, about how he was going to teach me how to dream big and show me how to achieve those dreams, was different than anything I'd ever heard before. I had no idea how we were going to make those things come true, but I knew that Malcolm would lead me there.

We agreed to meet after each group and talk. I would keep my copy of *The Greatest Miracle in the World* and review it daily. I would write down questions, any questions, as well as my dream list and bring them to Malcolm on Mondays.

Have fun.

~9~

MONDAYS

Mondays became the highlight of my week. The anticipation made time pass. Sometimes I had questions, but if I didn't, Malcolm and I just talked.

Over the next seven weeks, we developed a tight friendship. I spent my week reading or just thinking about the ideas Malcolm presented to me. On Mondays we would talk; we even laughed.

Malcolm had a way of showing new ideas to me, things that were so simple that I could understand them but so powerful that they changed my life.

Become a champion.

We eventually talked about each other. Malcolm learned about my background, why I was in jail, and my family. I told him how my mom worked double shifts as a waitress to help keep food on the table for me and my two younger brothers.

I learned a lot about Malcolm ~ about how he had worked hard to become rich and financially successful. He told me about his struggles with self-doubt and worry. I never would have guessed that Malcolm had any worries at all. He was always so confident.

One night I asked Malcolm about his business.

"I'm the CEO of my own company. Do you know what that means?"

"Yeah. It means that you're the one who makes all the money." I really didn't have any idea what a CEO does.

Malcolm chuckled. "Well, what it really means is that I am the leader of a company. It stands for chief executive officer. I am responsible for the company's success or failure."

"We need to take a look at your dream list. Do you have it with you?"

I carried that list with me everywhere. Every time I woke up I made sure that it was with me. I hadn't put it down since Malcolm and I started talking about it. But I

Repay favors.

was a little afraid to show it to him. *What if he laughs or tells me that I'm stupid?* I handed it to him anyway.

Malcolm smiled as he looked over my list. "Tony, I'm going to show you how to get everything on this list. Then we'll make a new list and I'll show you how to get everything on that list. Keep this until you get released."

"They could send me to prison, you know."

"Yes, they could. Either way you can keep it until you're released," Malcolm said, handing me back the list.

All I could say was okay. I'd make sure I had it when I made it to the outside.

I could hardly contain myself during my final meeting with Malcolm at the county jail.

"My lawyer visited me today," I said to Malcolm. "He said he spoke to the DA. I have a court date this Friday and the DA is going to ask the judge to let me out. I'm getting out on Friday! No more jail time!"

"That's great!" Then Malcolm asked me, "Are you ready to make the changes we have been talking about?"

"Yes. Definitely." Even while I was in jail, Malcolm had helped me grow. I really felt like a new person. "I will *never* be arrested again," I told him.

Don't assume anything.

Malcolm said, "Here's what we are going to do. On Saturday morning, the day you get out, I want you to meet me at the lighthouse on the east side of Lake Hefner to run. At 6:00 A.M."

I nodded. I was so excited that I almost didn't realize that Malcolm meant six *in the morning*. I didn't care. I had made a promise and knew that I would be there.

Malcolm said, "It's a little strange that this little lake has a genuine lighthouse. There are no ships on Lake Hefner, so the lighthouse is just for decoration. It was built a few years ago by developers, but it's great to use as a place to meet."

"I'll be there," I promised.

Friday finally came. I sat in my cell and waited for something to happen. I was excited about starting my new life. All the time I'd spent reading and meeting with Malcolm had shown me that my future held real possibilities. No more getaway cars for me.

A guard came, unlocked the door, and motioned me out of the cell. All of the other inmates stayed. This had to mean that I was going to court, just like my lawyer said.

Always be on time.

\approx10\approx

JUDGMENT

The guard took me down the hall to the elevator where we joined up with some other inmates. We were all handcuffed, shackled, and told to stand facing the back of the elevator. It was humiliating, like we were so hideous our faces shouldn't even be seen. We were taken to a garage and put in a transport van.

It took just five minutes to reach the unloading area of the courthouse. We shuffled to the elevator for inmates. It was near the back of the main corridor and no outsiders

Go to a seminar.

were allowed on it. The elevator took us to a jail at the top of the courthouse where they checked us in.

I was one of the first prisoners to be led out. Three other inmates were handcuffed to me and we were taken to the courtroom. The judge came into the room after we sat down. I hoped my attorney had told me the truth and that I would be going home tonight.

"All rise!" said one of the guards. Everyone in the room stood, and we then sat in unison as the judge said, "You may be seated."

"Will the defendant please come forward?" A guard tapped me on the shoulder. I was uncuffed from the other inmates and walked over to the bench. My court-appointed attorney met me there. He smiled and nodded at me.

"Sir, do you know why you are here?"

"Yes, ma'am," I replied. This time I actually did know.

"And why are we here?"

"It's the end of my ninety days, and you're gonna decide about me going to prison," I said.

"That's correct. Now, I've spoken to the DA, and I've also spoken to your lawyer. From what I understand, you have not been in any trouble in jail. I don't see any contact with the jail staff."

Take a walk.

"No, ma'am."

"Sir, the district attorney has filed a motion to dismiss application to revoke the suspended sentence. Based upon the information I have here, I am going to grant the dismissal. What this means is that once the paperwork is processed, you will be released."

"Yes, ma'am. Thank you." I was so relieved I almost fell down.

"Now don't get too excited." The judge took her glasses off and held them in her left hand. She paused. "I want to make something perfectly clear. You are getting a second chance. There will *NOT* be a third." The judge was using her left hand for emphasis. Each time she said an important word she pointed her glasses at me.

"If you come back before me with any trouble at all ～ and I mean *ANY* ～ and the DA files another application to revoke your suspended sentence, I will grant it. You will go to prison for the maximum amount of time allowed by law. Do you understand?"

"Yes, ma'am." This time I knew there would not be any more trouble. This was going to be the last time I appeared before this judge or any other.

Go to the park.

"You are excused." The judge signed some papers and handed them to one of the guards.

And with that I was on my way out. I didn't know how long it would take for the paperwork to process, but I did know that I would not wake up in jail tomorrow. I was escorted back to the other prisoners and handcuffed at the end of the line.

All of us were taken back to the jail, but I was left in the holding area.

I can't believe it! I'm really getting out of here tonight! All I could think about was taking a real shower, sleeping in a real bed, eating real food. I couldn't wait to get the stench of the jail off of me.

I sat in the holding area for some time. Each time a guard walked by the window I was certain it would be the one to bring me my street clothes and take me to the processing area. Each time the guard passed by.

Another inmate was brought in. I had seen him in the jail, but I didn't know who he was.

"Getting out?" asked the stranger.

"Yeah, just as soon as they process my papers."

"Don't be in too big of a hurry. Probably won't be until after midnight."

Finish strong.

My heart dropped. How was I going to last until midnight? The other inmate stretched out on a bench and fell asleep almost immediately.

Dinner came. I let my new cellmate eat my portion. "Even if I do get released after midnight, I can eat then." I couldn't stand the thought of another bologna sandwich.

I dozed off and woke up to the sound of the cell door sliding open. A guard walked in and called my name. "Time to go."

I opened my eyes and shook off the sleep. I walked out of the cell and made my way to the processing area. Another guard handed me a plastic bag that held all the belongings I arrived with: my wallet, some loose change, and the keys to Mom's house. It also had the book Malcolm had given me. I signed a sheet of paper stating I had received all of my possessions. Another guard handed me my street clothes.

I changed clothes and made my way down the hall. I stopped at a locked metal door and paused. Someone watching through a camera pressed a button and triggered the lock. I pushed on the door, took three steps, and turned left. I followed the corridor around to the main desk.

I showed the guard there the paperwork I had been

Read.

given. The guard nodded, motioned for me to come forward, and grabbed my left hand. The guard took it and used a rubber stamp to mark it.

I looked down. The mark said, "released." I smiled and walked to the front door, just a few feet away. I took the final step and went outside, no longer a prisoner.

I was not the same person I had been when I was locked up. Malcolm had taught me how to be a new person, and I had done everything I could to change in jail. But now I was on the outside. The changes I would make on the outside weren't just in my mind or thoughts. They would be in the way I acted. I had never been as excited about anything as I was about starting my new life.

As the jail's front door was closing, I glanced back to the main desk. The clock above it read 3:55.

Sharing is caring.

~11~

RUNNING

Only two hours until I was supposed to meet Malcolm. It was way too late to call anyone. No one, not even my mom, would be willing to meet me at this time of night. I was really hungry but decided that would have to wait. I had to walk, and that meant I had just enough time to make it to the lake. No way could I let myself be late. The opportunity awaiting me at the lighthouse was worth whatever price I had to pay to get there.

I walked to the curb and took a breath. The outside air

Don't blame others.

tasted almost sweet. I took two more deep breaths and began walking north.

I could have saved time by cutting through neighborhoods, but I wasn't going to take the chance. *No way I'm going to be caught in a neighborhood at four in the morning. I have a felony conviction for burglary and just got out of the county jail.*

If someone saw me, got the wrong idea, and called the police, I would have to explain why I was there. It would cost me valuable time. So I stuck to the well-lit main road even though it would take longer.

I walked as quickly as I could because I didn't have any time to spare. My stomach was rumbling, but the only thing I could think about was getting to the lake and keeping the promise I made to Malcolm.

I didn't own a watch to check my progress. That made keeping up a fast pace even more important. If I didn't make it on time, it wouldn't be because of lack of effort.

It was really quiet. Occasionally a dog would bark or a car would pass. Other than that, it was just me and my footsteps. Eventually a fast food restaurant sign revealed my progress. Its big electronic clock told me that it was just one minute after five. I pushed myself to keep going. With

Focus.

the same effort it took to get me to this point, I would meet Malcolm just on time.

Familiar landmarks appeared, grew bigger, and then disappeared as I went by.

I reached May Avenue and turned right. Almost there. The long walk was taking its toll. My breathing was heavy. My shirt was covered with sweat.

A few more blocks and I would be at the lake. Then I could wind my way along the east side toward the lighthouse.

I forced my feet onward and maintained my pace. I found the path on the south side of the lake and followed it. In the distance I saw the outline of the lighthouse.

I kept going. When I reached the lighthouse, I finally relaxed and looked around. I saw a car turn off the cross street and enter the parking lot. The car parked and the driver got out.

I knew it was Malcolm. I had come to know him well enough that I could recognize his walk as he made his way toward the lighthouse. And who else would be out here at six on a Saturday morning?

Malcolm reached the lighthouse and I was standing at the base in the glow of a street lamp.

Exercise your mind.

"Morning, Tony. Good to see you."

"Hey."

I was still out of breath from the walk and my shirt was sticking to my skin. I couldn't help but think that it would have been nice for Malcolm to have arranged a ride for me. But it didn't matter. Malcolm and I were both here and I was thrilled at what could possibly unfold.

My stomach growled. I regretted not eating dinner.

Malcolm was dressed even more casually than he had been during group. He wore a faded T-shirt, shorts, and running shoes.

"Thanks for being here on time. This is one of my favorite places. I do most of my best thinking here.

"Tony, there are several different parts to you. Man is mental, physical, and spiritual. Exercise is one of the most important things we can do. If you can run, swim, or cycle twenty to thirty minutes four times a week, it will have a huge impact on your life. Exercise keeps you in good shape, reduces stress, and helps you to feel better about yourself. It increases your self-esteem and it doesn't cost much. You can do it outside and get fresh air. And you can even do it with other people to improve friendships."

Malcolm paused and I was struck by the quiet. After

Be slow to anger.

being locked up in the county jail for three months, I felt like I had landed on another planet. There was always noise in jail, and being here where it was silent and peaceful was almost overwhelming.

"I've got something for you." He motioned to me, and we went to his car. He pulled out his keys and popped the trunk open. It was empty except for a plastic sack. Malcolm reached in and pulled out a pair of running shoes.

"Put these on," Malcolm said as he handed me the shoes.

I looked at the shoes. They were brand new, and not the cheap shoes from the discount shoe store. They were nice, name-brand shoes — like the ones I'd seen at the expensive shoe place in the mall. They must have cost at least a hundred bucks. I never thought I would own a pair of shoes like that, and I never expected anyone to give me such a great gift.

"What are these for?"

"Let's go for a run."

"A run? Malcolm, I just walked all the way...."

"I know. You'll be good and loose."

Malcolm and I had talked about exercise while I was in jail. We had even talked about going for a run on the day

Be honest.

that I got out. But I really didn't expect Malcolm to hold me to that. Not after I had such a long night.

I sat on the rear bumper of Malcolm's car. I took off my old shoes and put on the new ones. The old ones went into the shoebox and that went back into the trunk along with my book.

Malcolm jogged south down the running path and I followed. I had no idea how long I'd be able to keep up.

There was no noise to disturb us except the sound of our shoes hitting the ground ~ well, that and the sound of my own breathing. I had never done this type of exercise and my lungs were doing double time to make up for years of inactivity. As far as I could tell, Malcolm had not taken a breath since he got here. He was in really good shape.

The trail gently curved. We were near the parking lot I had entered on my way to the lighthouse. We jogged for at least a mile more before we reached another parking lot. There was a truck sitting there and someone was waiting in it. As we got closer, I could see it was Gary, the guy I had met in jail. He had come with Malcolm on several occasions. I heard the door close and watched him jog toward us.

"Good morning, Gary."

Give freely.

"Morning, Malcolm."

"Gary, this is Tony. I think you two met in group."

"Hey, man. How ya doing?" Gary nodded at me and we continued the run.

"Great," I replied. How else would I be at 6:00 A.M. on a Saturday after I had walked for two hours on an empty stomach? I was excited to be here but the toll of my night was beginning to affect me. I should have eaten dinner, even if it was a bologna sandwich.

No one spoke for a while. After about a half-mile, Malcolm broke the silence. "Gary, how's the business? Dig any good holes lately?"

I laughed, but Gary later told me it was the same question Malcolm used every week. Gary managed a smile.

"It's going great. Remember the job that I was telling you about last week? I put in a bid and got it."

"Really? That's awesome. Have you started yet?"

"No, I just found out yesterday. We start digging first thing Monday."

"Tony, Gary owns his own backhoe business. Just what, eighteen months ago, Gary was in jail. He got released and didn't own any equipment other than a shovel. Now he

Creation, not competition.

has his own business with five employees," Malcolm explained.

Gary said, "Well, six, and that's one of the things that I wanted to talk to you about."

I did my best to listen. My legs burned and my stomach rumbled. I strained to focus on the words.

"With this new job I feel like I need more employees and maybe some more equipment. To do that I would need to either take out some of the money I've been setting aside or borrow the money. I'm not sure what to do."

"Don't do either," Malcolm answered before his next step. "The money you've set aside is your reserve. It's for rainy days or emergencies only. Getting a new job is not an emergency, it's an opportunity. Leave that money alone. And as for borrowing the money, you're a small business owner. You don't need the pressure of a loan payment each month."

I could tell Gary was listening. All I could think about was how difficult the run had become. They seemed to run with no effort at all.

"There has to be another solution using your existing manpower and capital. You may not see it yet, but it's there." Malcolm spoke with confidence, but he wasn't

Do important things first.

cocky or arrogant. All of his answers seemed to make sense. I could tell he had a lot of knowledge.

"Gary, I want you to get a book called *The E-Myth Revisited* by Michael Gerber. It will help you run your business. It's a simple book, but anyone who runs a business should read it. It will help you set up a plan so that you can run your business smoothly."

"How do you know so much?" I asked Malcolm.

"I read. By reading you gain knowledge. If you take action with knowledge, you get a lot out of life and can make a difference in the world. And if you don't have money to buy books, you can use the library. Our libraries are full of the greatest books in the world."

"Yeah, but the only people who read at my school were bookworms, the goody-two-shoes."

"That's kid stuff, Tony. If you want to be successful in life, read."

The trail kept changing directions. Why couldn't it just be straight? We passed a fire station and then I could see a golf course on both sides. The course was empty. It was too early even for golfers.

My legs hurt and I had a hard time keeping up. Malcolm and Gary slowed their pace slightly. I did my best to

Carry a book with you.

fight through the pain. We made it to the far west side of the lake. The trail merged into a city street. On the left hand side were houses; on the right, there was a brick wall, rock shoreline, and then the water.

"Tony, where are you going to live?" Malcolm asked.

"I'm...not...sure." I spat out between breaths. My plan had been to take care of that when I was released from jail, but because I got out so late, I didn't know.

I knew I could live with my mom. She would never turn me away. But I didn't want to go there. I didn't want any more favors. I am a grown man, nineteen years old, and should be able to take care of myself. Going back to live with Mom would almost be like admitting that life was going to be just the same. *The next time I see my mom I want her to know I have changed, that I have a plan, and that I am improving my life. I want her to have a different look than she did when I saw her in the courtroom.*

"Gary, you've got a spare bedroom, don't you?" Malcolm asked.

"Yes."

The pain in my legs was really starting to bother me. I could just barely hear what was happening.

Always do your best.

"Is it all right if Tony stays with you a few months until he gets on his feet?"

"That would be fine."

We kept jogging. I wasn't sure what had just happened. I trusted Malcolm but didn't know Gary at all. I wasn't comfortable living with someone I didn't know very well.

As I struggled with what to do, a calm came over me. I thought of all the Monday nights we had spent together and all of the things that Malcolm had taught me. I knew I could count on Malcolm and that he would not steer me wrong. My concern over living with Gary disappeared.

"Does that work for you, Tony?"

It took me a moment to get the air to be able to answer. "Yes." Living with Gary for a little while was a much better option than explaining to my mom what I had done and what I was going to do.

I started to wonder how much further I could jog. I would have thrown up miles ago, but my stomach was too empty. We began the stretch of road on the north side of the lake. Each time my foot landed I could feel the jar through my entire body. Each step felt like I was dragging lead.

I could see the lighthouse on the east side of the lake. I

Develop routine.

hoped the end would not be far off. A few cars were moving into the parking lot and the signs of life were reassuring.

"Tony, where are you going to work?"

It was another question that had to be answered but I hadn't thought much about it. I really didn't have any idea of what I was going to do.

Malcolm didn't wait for an answer. "This week I want you to go out and find a job. There are a bunch of places within walking distance from Gary's house. Be sure to read each day. The three of us will meet next Saturday at the same time. You can tell me about your job then."

I nodded. I was so busy breathing, I could not get a word out. It took all my energy to keep moving. I focused on the far side of the lake. We were getting closer to the lighthouse. No one talked. All I could hear was the plodding of our feet and the pounding of my heart.

We reached the far side of the lake together. The road weaved south and went through a parking lot. On this side of the lake there were water fountains and benches. I would have done anything to be able to sit and drink. After all, I hadn't sat down in hours.

The trail emerged from the parking lot and headed

Drink water.

south. Other people were out now; some were getting ready to run, some walking, and some riding bikes.

I focused on the lighthouse. I knew we would reach it soon.

I desperately hoped that would be the end. I was lucky to have made it this far. I couldn't imagine anyone wanting to do more than one lap around the lake. I had heard about people who ran really long distances for fun. I was starting to think they were crazy.

Somehow I managed to keep my legs moving. When we reached the lighthouse and stopped, I was thrilled. But not just because we'd stopped. I felt incredible and I couldn't believe what I'd just done.

Wow! I just ran around the lake. If I can do this, what can't I do? I thought. *It's amazing what I can do if I just take the action. I could never have done this run alone though. It's great to have someone to do it with. I'm glad I don't have to be alone.*

For a moment, I recalled how I felt when I first met Malcolm — about how I started to dream and believe that I could do great things.

Malcolm and Gary slowed and started walking to Malcolm's car. I followed. I couldn't help but notice the car. It

Accept responsibility.

was a blue, four-door Lexus. The interior was tan leather. I could see that the car was clean, inside and out.

Gary noticed me looking at the car.

"Nice car, huh?" Gary said. "Malcolm taught me the secret of buying cars. Find a nice used one that the previous owner has taken care of. Then make sure you maintain it, too."

Malcolm nodded. "Winners don't have the best of everything. They take the best care of what they have."

Inside the car were three bottles of water and some bananas. Malcolm handed me and Gary one of each and kept one for himself.

I tore open the banana and ate it in two bites. I chugged half of the bottle of water. I would have eaten anything to fill my stomach.

"Man, I'm starved. I haven't eaten since lunch yesterday." I was able to get out between breaths.

"You didn't have dinner?" Gary asked.

I shook my head no and gulped down the rest of the water. "I gave my dinner to some dude in the cell with me. Figured I could eat dinner on the outside. Didn't know I would be in there until four in the morning."

Malcolm looked at me. "You walked all the way out

Stick to your plan.

here and then went on a nine-mile run with no dinner or breakfast?"

"Yes, sir."

"Tony, I do a lot of meetings. Some of the people listen, very few read any of the books I hand out, but even fewer meet me on the outside. People that show this kind of commitment on the first day and stick with it are successful. If you apply that kind of effort to everything you do, you'll be unstoppable."

"Good run," Gary offered while gulping his water. "I feel awesome."

"Great. Good job guys." Malcolm looked at me. "Tony, one of the things I want you to learn is that exercise is one of the most important things in your life. People that have self-esteem do esteemable things."

Gary and Malcolm high-fived each other. Malcolm went back to his car, opened the trunk, and handed me the shoebox with my old shoes in it. He also brought out a book and handed it to me.

"Tony, one of the most important things in life is how to deal with people. And you need to get to know the right people. This book will help." He handed me a new copy of

Invite someone to church.

How to Win Friends and Influence People by Dale Carnegie. "I want you to read this by next week."

"Thank you."

Malcolm always knew just what to do. I had wondered what to read next. I liked the other book that he had given me, but I had read it so many times I almost knew it by heart. His timing could not have been better.

"Guys, get in the car. Let's go have breakfast at my place."

Enjoy church.

12

GARY

We got in the car and minutes later we pulled up to a beautiful rock home near the lake in a neighborhood I had never seen before. Two huge doors opened to the home's entryway, and to the right I saw the dining room. Beyond that there appeared to be a living room with a view of the lake. I could even see the lighthouse. The house was cleaner than anywhere I had ever been. The air felt cool and crisp.

Two girls ran up and hugged Malcolm around the knees.

Be a greeter at church.

"Daddy!" they both yelled.

"Tony, these are my daughters. This is Emily; she's six, and Abby is five." They waved at me from behind their father's legs. Malcolm patted them both on the back.

"Hey, honey." An attractive blonde woman walked in from another room. She was a little shorter than Malcolm. She walked up to him and gave him a kiss and a hug.

"Tony, this is my wife, Leslie. Leslie, this is Tony."

She smiled at me. "Nice to meet you, Tony. Gary, how are you?"

"Fine."

"You boys must be starving. Come on in. There's breakfast waiting for you in the dining room," Leslie said. The kids ran to the dining table and sat down.

We ate scrambled eggs, sausage, biscuits, and jam. The smell of such good food after being in jail almost made my nose explode. It was the best breakfast that I'd ever had. Not just because the food was good and I was starving but also because of the company. It was fun watching Malcolm and Leslie.

They really enjoyed being together. As we talked during the meal, Malcolm and Leslie smiled at each other and laughed. Occasionally, one would lean over and

Run four days a week.

whisper something to the other. It was like watching two best friends.

I started thinking about my own family. My mom was great. She gave us kids everything she had. But my dad never came to see us much. He didn't even pay child support. I sure couldn't remember a time when my parents had still been together and they'd been affectionate with one another. I decided I was going to learn as much as I could from Malcolm so that if I ever got married and started a family, my home would be happy like his.

After we ate, Malcolm drove us back to the parking lot. Gary and I got out and said good-bye to Malcolm.

It hit me that Malcolm had it all. He had a beautiful family, a home, and a growing business. He was in great shape and ran marathons. I knew I had to learn as much as I could from him. If I achieved only half as much as he had, I still would exceed my wildest dreams.

When we reached the parking lot, Gary went over to a shiny pickup and pushed a button on his key. I saw the parking lights flash and heard the locks open. The truck was clean inside and out and I knew it had been well maintained.

I got in on the passenger side. I had never been in such

Reconciliation, not retaliation.

a nice truck. I couldn't believe that it was owned by someone like me. Just eighteen months ago, Gary had been an inmate.

If Gary can get all of this, so can I. I'm willing to take whatever action I have to, I thought as Gary backed out of the parking space.

Gary drove for ten minutes before pulling into a neighborhood and then into a driveway. He pushed a button in an overhead compartment. One of the two garage doors opened.

I looked at Gary. "Is this yours?"

"Yes. Just me and the bank."

My jaw dropped.

"I know, Tony. Sometimes I don't believe it myself. All I can say is that Malcolm is a great teacher and mentor. He's a great person. Listen to what he says. Do what he tells you to do. You never know what can happen to you."

Gary drove into the garage. I opened my door and followed Gary into the house. The garage led into the laundry room and then into the kitchen.

"There's food in the fridge. Your room is down at the end of the hall. The bathroom is on the right. Clean towels are in the cabinet."

Be a person of value.

Gary went down the hall and I heard a door close. I looked around the house and noticed how clean it was. Nothing was out of place, and there was no clutter. I walked down the hall to my room. An hour later I was asleep.

When I woke up, it was 1:30 in the afternoon. My legs were a little sore but I managed to get to the living room. Gary was sitting on the sofa reading the book that Malcolm told him to read.

Gary obviously takes action, I thought. *No wonder he has a house and a nice truck and owns a business.*

Gary saw me walking a little stiffly into the room and chuckled. "Don't worry. It gets better," he said as he closed the book. "Be sure to wash your clothes this afternoon. Detergent is on top of the washer."

"Okay."

I went to the kitchen, made my lunch, and leaned against the counter to eat it. I didn't even bother to sit down because I knew if I did I might not be able to get up. Gary found some clean clothes for me to wear while I washed my own.

I changed my clothes, started the laundry, and made

Value people.

another sandwich. I could have eaten almost anything, but a sandwich was the least complicated and I didn't have the energy to think about cooking. I finished the sandwich and headed toward my room. Gary was on the couch reading again.

It felt so good to stretch out on my bed and be alone with my thoughts. No more cellmates. I thought about all that had happened in the last twenty-four hours. I was released from jail and able to get to the lake and meet Malcolm. I kept my promises. Everything that Malcolm and I talked about for the past several weeks was coming true.

I knew I was starting a new journey. My life wouldn't be like it had been before those ninety days in jail. I felt hope and peace like I never had before. I knew there was a purpose to my life and that I would do great things. I fell asleep wondering where the next twenty-four hours would take me.

Be loyal.

~13~

FELONY

I was up by 8:30 on Sunday and headed to the kitchen for breakfast.

When Gary got up, I said, "Gary, I just want to say thank you for letting me...." And that was as far as I could get. I was too grateful to finish the thought. It was overwhelming how Gary had opened his home to me. I was a complete stranger, but he had given me a place to live and food to eat.

"You're welcome. Trust me, I have been where you are. I'm glad to help. When you get the chance, and it may

Say what you mean.

come sooner than you think, you'll be able to do the same for someone else. Remember, being able to help someone is an honor and a privilege."

We didn't talk much for the rest of the day. I read and then spent the afternoon watching TV. I ate dinner and went to bed early because Monday I would start my job search. I wanted to have good news to tell Malcolm on Saturday.

On Monday morning, I felt a bit fearful. I needed to find a job. I really didn't like interviews — some stranger asking me stupid questions, like whether or not I have a pleasant personality or if I'm hardworking and honest. Doesn't everybody answer those questions the way they think the interviewer wants to hear them? I didn't know how or where, but I had to find a job today.

I was out the door by 9:00 A.M. Gary had gone to work earlier and I was on foot. Walking didn't bother me today. I was too excited. Malcolm was right. Within walking distance were many fast-food restaurants and convenience stores. I went into the nearest restaurant.

I smiled at the clerk and stood up straight.

"Can I help you?" asked the face behind the counter.

Believe in others.

"I want to apply for a job." I looked her right in the eyes. I was more confident than I had ever been.

The clerk looked under the counter and opened a drawer. She pulled out an application and a pen and handed both to me.

"Fill this out. Bring it back to me, and I will have the manager meet with you."

It took me ten minutes. I had written down Gary's address and phone number to use. I felt fine until I reached the back of the form and saw the question that read, "Have you ever been convicted of a felony?" I checked the "Yes" box. My confidence dropped a little bit, but I wasn't too concerned. I had done my time. That part of my life was over. I reviewed my answers and gave the form and pen back to the clerk.

"Have a seat. The manager will be out in a few minutes." I thanked her and bought a drink. The clerk disappeared into the back of the restaurant.

I sat down. Just as I finished my drink another woman came out from behind the counter. She was carrying the application and made her way to my table. She introduced herself as the manager and sat down.

"Okay, let's get started. Everything seems to be in order

Impact the lives of others.

here." Her eyes were moving side to side as she read my application. She eventually made it to the second page. Near the bottom was the question about being convicted of a crime.

"So you have a felony conviction?" She put the paper down.

I was expecting this. I had even rehearsed my answer. I started to explain. "Yes, ma'am. I was very young and I made a mistake. It's something..."

"I'm sorry. We have a company policy. I can't hire anyone with a felony conviction. Good luck." She stood up and went behind the counter as quickly as she had come.

I was stunned, not at being turned down, but at how quickly it had happened. It was as though once she found out, I didn't exist anymore. Like I wasn't a real person. I quietly left for the next restaurant.

By the end of the day I had heard every reason for rejection possible.

"Sorry. Not hiring."

"Great. We'll call you when we make our decision."

"Don't think you'd be suited for the opening we have right now."

Mean what you say.

More often than not, it was just, "We don't hire people with a felony conviction."

I went back to Gary's house dejected. Gary wasn't home from work yet and I had the house to myself. All my earlier confidence was shattered.

I can't believe it. No one will give me a job. I had more hope while I was locked up than I do right now.

I was beginning to doubt all that Malcolm and I had talked about. Was any of it true? Had I believed a lie?

I walked back to my room and picked up my copy of *How to Win Friends and Influence People*. I started to read. I thought about all the things that had happened in the last several weeks. The peace I had come to know returned.

As I started to read the book, I thought about new possibilities. Instead of thinking about the failure of applying for a job, I thought about taking action. As long as I took action, I would find a job and be successful. I looked around Gary's house and saw the rewards of a focused person taking action. If he could do it, I could too.

Read more.

~14~

DIGGING HOLES

Gary made it home later. I was still sitting on the sofa with the book in my hand.

"How did it go today? Any luck?" Gary asked.

I shook my head. "Not today. Maybe tomorrow."

"Too bad. Feel like grilling some burgers?"

Gary opened the freezer, took out two frozen patties, and headed for the back porch. We ate at the kitchen table.

Gary broke the silence. "Tony, I know today was tough. Malcolm can show you what to do, but you have to be the

Be polite.

one to take the action. There are no free lunches. You are going to have challenges. Do you understand?"

I understood. "Yeah, it just wasn't easy. I really thought I would get a chance somewhere."

"You will. Just keep plugging along."

We washed the dishes together and then headed off to our separate rooms. I read and prepared myself for another day of job hunting. I wasn't going to let one bad day keep me from taking the action I needed to be successful.

I was up by seven on Tuesday morning. I met Gary in the kitchen. He was rinsing the remains of his scrambled eggs off his plate. I made my way to the cabinet and grabbed a box of cereal. After I had my first bite, Gary spoke.

"Tony, I have an idea. You need a job, and I need more workers. Do you want to work for me?"

I didn't need any time to think. "Yes."

Gary said, "Malcolm was right. There was a simple answer. I can't believe I didn't see it before."

I was almost stunned. I had gotten a job and wasn't even finished with breakfast. At this rate I might be a millionaire by lunch.

We were both relieved that our problems had been

Accept challenges.

quickly resolved for our mutual good. Within an hour we were headed for the job site.

At the site Gary parked his truck and greeted the other workers. He introduced me and we all shook hands. Gary pulled me aside and took me back to the truck. In the bed was an old, beat up shovel. Gary handed it to me.

"Take care of this," Gary said with a smile. "This is the same one I started with when I got out of jail. It doesn't look like much, but it's one of my most prized possessions. Brought it out of retirement just for you."

I looked at the shovel and then at Gary. I wasn't sure if Gary was serious or not, but I decided I'd better treat that shovel with care.

"Go get in line with the other guys. They'll show you what to do."

I made my way to the other workers and followed their instructions. I dug my way to lunch and then to dinner. After we quit for the day, I put the shovel in the back of Gary's truck and we headed home.

We continued this routine for the rest of the week. Each day we drove to the site, Gary inspected his backhoe and dug, and I dug with the other guys. Gary and I shared

Defeat challenges.

breakfast and dinner together, and we were becoming fast friends.

I was amazed at how far Gary had come since he had gotten out of jail. And Gary told me how he was impressed with my hard work and good attitude. After all he had done for me, there was no way I was going to let him down. I was going to work as hard as I could. Gary gave me my first paycheck on Friday. We both felt a sense of pride.

As I stepped back, paycheck in hand, one of the other workers, Lance, approached Gary. Lance seemed nervous. I was standing by the truck and could see everything. Gary listened to Lance, nodded, and then responded. I knew enough to tell it was a tough conversation.

After several minutes, Gary smiled and politely shook Lance's hand. Gary came back to the truck. Lance went to his car where two of the other diggers were waiting. They loaded into Lance's car and disappeared.

"What was that?" I was curious and asked Gary as soon as his door closed.

Gary took a deep breath. "Well, Lance just told me that he is quitting. He's starting his own company, and two of my other employees are going with him."

Get a mentor.

I couldn't believe that anyone would want to quit working for Gary. In the short time I had known him, Gary had been fair and honest. I had worked at places where the boss barked orders and then disappeared, leaving the "workers" to get the dirty work done — no matter how ridiculous the request had been. One of the things I liked best about Gary was the fact that Gary was willing to do whatever it took to get the job done. Gary was often right next to me, shovel in hand. And Gary never complained or criticized. I'd asked Gary why he digs, too.

"Having that shovel in my hand is a reminder of how much I have and how far I have come. It really makes me grateful," he'd said.

But right now Gary didn't seem grateful. He was disappointed. "And besides those three quitting, Lance told me he got his first job. It was one I had bid on."

Gary started the truck and headed home, lost in thought. I wasn't sure what to say, and the ride home was silent.

At the house Gary finally spoke up. "We need to get to bed early. We meet Malcolm tomorrow for our run."

"Oh, yeah." I had almost forgotten. I wanted to see

Be a friend.

Malcolm and tell him about my job, but right now I was worried about my friend Gary.

Keep your promises.

～15～

LANCE

Gary and I made it to the lighthouse on Saturday morning. Malcolm was waiting for us. "Morning, gentlemen."

We waited for Malcolm to start and began jogging beside him. We headed west, the same way we had last week.

Malcolm started with his usual joke. "Gary, how's business? Dig any good holes lately?"

Gary forced a smile. "Good and bad."

"Okay, give me the bad news first," Malcolm said without missing a beat.

Be kind.

"Well, one of my employees, Lance, told me yesterday that he's quitting to start his own company. I can understand that. But what really upsets me is that he is taking two of my other employees with him. He never discussed this. And to top it off, he's already got a job lined up. It's one that I had bid on. Lance helped me with the figures and I know that's how he got the job. He knew just what to bid to undercut me."

Gary's escalating voice told me that he was getting upset. When he stopped talking, his jaw clenched. Gary's arms were normally relaxed and his hands were open, but now his arms were stiff and his fists were clenched.

Malcolm could also see how Gary was feeling.

"Gary, life is not fair. Things like this will happen. You will have challenges."

Gary kept running and his feet were pounding against the ground as if he were trying to beat the anger out of his body.

Malcolm continued, "You can get angry and hold on to this. If you do that, it will hold you back. Trust me, it takes a lot of energy to be angry about something. You can be right or you can be happy. Sometimes it's better to let the little things go so that you can be happy."

Go the extra mile.

Gary was listening and getting angrier by the step.

"Or, you can accept the fact that this has happened and move forward. You can get bitter or you can get better. I know how difficult this is. I'm not saying it will be easy, but letting go is the better way."

No response came from Gary, so Malcolm continued talking. "Gary, I had a very similar thing happen to me. Some of my employees left my business and started their own. They operate just down the street from my building.

"And there's one more thing. Do whatever you can to help Lance become more successful."

"*Help him?* Why would I want to help him?" Gary said as he forced his body down the path.

Needless to say, Gary didn't look too interested in helping Lance.

Malcolm continued. "Yes, Gary, I said help him. We're here to make a positive difference in the world. The more people we help, the better our lives will be. Now let's end this on a happy note. What's the good news?"

Gary took a moment and then motioned his head toward me. "I'd like for you to meet my new employee."

"You hired Tony? Good move. How do you like your new boss?"

Be frugal.

"He's great."

I meant it. I really did like working for Gary. It was one of the best things to ever happen to me.

"How did this happen?"

"Well, I tried to find a job at some of the fast food places and stores like you said. But no one would give me a chance. It was really frustrating."

Malcolm asked, "Remember what we talked about after you read the book for the first time? About how you are special and there is a purpose to your life?"

"Yes."

"Tony, no one is going to give you a job. You have to go out and find work that needs to be done. You have to create opportunity."

We kept heading east along the jogging trail. I wasn't having as difficult a time keeping up as I did last week. We were able to stay together much more easily.

"Gary, aren't you glad you didn't take that money out of your savings?"

"Yeah," said Gary with a quick laugh. "You were right again, Malcolm."

"Having that money set aside is important. And you should not touch it, except for something really important.

Thank people.

I just knew that some other solution would come along. It always does."

I was able to follow the conversation much better this week. I was convinced that Malcolm knew a lot. He seemed to have wisdom, and he was open to sharing his knowledge with Gary and me.

We ran the same course we had last week, but to me it seemed new. Last week I had been too busy forcing my legs to move to see the details of where I was. This time I was able to see a pair of fishermen sitting on the bank of the lake and a foursome getting ready to hit the golf course.

We were on the west side of the lake now. I was beginning to enjoy the experience.

"Tony, there's something important I want you to do," Malcolm said.

"Yes, sir." I understood that whatever Malcolm told me to do would help me.

"This week, after you get paid, I want you to go to the bank. You need to take 10 percent of your paycheck and open a savings account. Whenever you get paid, you take 10 percent of that and put it in your account. In other words, ten cents of every dollar goes into a savings account. Do you understand?"

Use positive words.

I nodded.

"You need to leave that money alone. There are going to be times when you think you need to take that money out, but don't do it. Don't spend it on anything without talking to me about it first.

"You heard how Gary thought he needed to take out some of his savings. Then he found another solution. Just remember, you can always find another way to resolve your problem other than taking money out of savings."

"Okay." I was happy to do it. If Malcolm said it was important and Gary was doing it, so would I.

We continued north along the west side of the lake and then followed the trail east. I saw a large wooded park on the left side of the dam, something else I had not noticed last week. As we went further west, I could see kites flying. Whoever was flying them was near the boat club.

Malcolm, Gary, and I kept the same pace. No one had to slow down this time. We hit the east side and stayed on the trail until it ran into the parking lot by the lighthouse. I followed Malcolm and Gary to Malcolm's car. We stopped and once again Malcolm reached into his Lexus and pulled out bananas and water. We drank and snacked without much talk.

Remember your victories.

Malcolm gave me another book. This one was called *Think and Grow Rich* by Napoleon Hill.

"Tony, part of being a successful business owner is having the proper attitude. This book will help you get and keep the right attitude toward success."

I took the book and thanked him.

"Well, it's time to go," Malcolm said after checking his watch. He shook hands with Gary and me and left.

Gary said this had been Malcolm's routine for years — to run at 6:00 A.M. on Saturday at the lighthouse on Lake Hefner. Malcolm had routine in his life, but he never seemed bored. All kinds of things were changing in Malcolm's life. His family was growing, he had new friends, his business was expanding, and he got to travel and take vacations to different places. Even with all this change, he always kept routine. Malcolm was, and still is, the most interesting person I have ever met.

Gary and I walked back to Gary's truck. Gary had been silent for some time and he didn't speak until we were almost home.

"Good run, huh, Tony?"

I could tell that Gary was talking just to make conversation. His mind was far away.

What gets measured gets improved.

"I guess I have to find some way to help Lance," he said.

Once we reached the house, Gary made a phone call.

"Yes, sir, this is Gary. I put in a bid on the job you've got Monday. I'm calling about Lance, the guy who did get the job."

I couldn't believe what I was hearing. Was Gary about to badmouth Lance after Malcolm had told him to help?

"Well, I just wanted you to know that he's worked for me the last year."

Here it comes, I thought.

Gary continued, "He's a great worker. Really dependable. You made a good decision in hiring him."

There was another pause while the person on the other end of the line spoke.

"Well, I just wanted to tell you this because I know it's his first job. He's going to do a great job for you.... Yes, sir. You have a great day."

Gary hung up the phone and walked into the living room. I could see how relieved he was. It was the most relaxed Gary had looked since he and Lance had talked.

Gary sighed, made something to eat, and sat down at the table to eat.

Stick to your plan.

On Sunday morning I was awake and ready by 8:00 A.M. The only problem was that I didn't have anywhere to go. After making some cereal I read. My mind was clean and alert, more so than I could ever remember.

Gary came to the kitchen and ate a quick breakfast. He told me he had errands to run.

I sat and thought while Gary was out. I had become so much happier since I had met Malcolm, but I wasn't sure why.

Then it hit me. For the first time in my life, I felt like there was someone who cared about me and had a plan for me — that there was someone who was not only going to tell me how to be successful but would also show me. Malcolm was going to give me the same guidance that he'd been giving Gary, and, with the same effort, I could be successful like Gary. For the first time in my life, I had a mentor. This realization gave me peace.

Gary returned that afternoon. He and I were both in good spirits.

"Man, I feel great!" I could hardly contain my enthusiasm. "My body feels great, and my brain — it's like somebody took it out and cleaned it."

Gary laughed. "It's the running. When you run, your

Enjoy new things.

body releases chemicals called endorphins. The word *endorphins* comes from the word *morphine*, which tells you endorphins are pretty powerful. That's why you feel so good."

"Cool." I didn't know I was a walking pharmacy.

Gary smiled and continued, "If you run four times a week at a reasonable pace, for thirty minutes at a time, you will feel like that all the time.

"Malcolm and I run every Tuesday, Wednesday, Thursday, and Saturday. The Saturday run is together, but the other three days we run by ourselves."

I had seen Gary leave the job site early on a few days and now I knew why. I decided right then I would run three days a week by myself, too.

Save 10 percent.

~16~

ACTION

Three months after my release from jail, I was well underway on my new path. Life was good. Just by reading, running, and being with people who want to achieve goals, my life had completely turned around. For the first time in my life, I was happy with the person I was becoming. Not one of the guys I met in jail would have recognized me. Gary and Malcolm wouldn't recognize me either if they hadn't been there to see the change.

I'd developed my own routine over the last few months. Each day after I woke up, I reviewed the books Malcolm

Share good news.

gave me. Then I did one hundred push-ups. I ran four days a week, three days by myself and Saturdays with Gary and Malcolm. I got paid on Friday, and by Tuesday I deposited at least 10 percent of my paycheck into my savings account. Following the routine Malcolm helped me set up was the difference between achieving the goals we talked about and not doing anything with my life.

I hadn't missed a single run. I welcomed the challenge of running instead of fearing it. A lap around the lake was not a problem anymore.

I still worked for Gary, and three months of labor had reshaped my body. There was no fat to be found and my arms were well toned.

I'd changed on the inside as well. I was no longer the child who went to jail — the one who was unwilling to accept any responsibility for my actions or plan for my future. I now understood the importance of taking the right kind of action, and I was full of hope and dreams.

I started visiting my mom. I called when I first got out, just to let her know where I was living and working. After two months I went to visit her. She was shocked to see how I had changed.

Be a giver.

I pulled a roll of cash from my pocket. "This is to start paying you back for the bail on my burglary charge."

I didn't wait for her to say anything, I just kept talking. "I also want you to know that I've been thinking about things. When Jeff and I got arrested for stealing beer, I was mad at him. I thought it was all his fault. But the truth is, I made a really bad decision to go along with him. It was my fault.

"Because I made such a bad choice, I wasted three months of my life in jail. I also embarrassed you and caused you a lot of pain.

"I just want you to know that I'm really sorry for doing that to you. But I'm learning a lot by reading and listening to my mentor, Malcolm. I'm learning to do things differently and I'm going to be a better person. You will never have to worry about me going to jail again."

My mom began crying, not the tears of disappointment like she had at the courthouse, but tears of pride, knowing that I was growing up. Every week since then I have gone to visit and pay her back.

Avoid self-doubt.

~17~

TEN %

Malcolm and I had been talking about financial responsibility and I started thinking about how I could make more money. I raised the subject with Malcolm during our Saturday run.

"Malcolm, I really like working for Gary. He's a great guy and has been more than fair with me. I don't want to quit, but I need to make more money. Can you help me?"

Malcolm thought for a moment. "Tony, you will only make a few dollars an hour with a shovel in your hand. To

Play by the rules.

make more money, you have to make yourself more valuable. That's why it is so important for you to read.

"Do you remember what you looked like when you got out of jail? You looked like you'd never lifted anything heavier than a toothbrush. Now you've got those muscles because you've been using them. Your brain is the same way. If you use it, it will grow and you will become more valuable."

I focused as hard as I could.

"You need to talk to Gary to let him know what is going on. Make sure he understands that you are not quitting. You can start your own business on the side. That's how you will make more money."

I couldn't believe Malcolm said this. Before I started working for Gary, I could barely hold a job, much less start my own business.

"Start my own business? Malcolm, I have a felony conviction. I couldn't get anyone other than Gary to hire me. How am I going to start my own business?"

"Well, Tony, we'll have to think of something that you can start small and then build up ~ something that doesn't cost a lot of money to start.

"Remember, Gary started with a shovel and now he has

Use kind words.

equipment and people working for him. And I started with just $62.53 and I've been able to turn that into a multimillion dollar business."

Malcolm paused. "Here's what we'll do. This time of year in Oklahoma, people need their yards mowed. I'll buy you a lawnmower and you can mow yards in the evenings and on Saturdays. You can pay me back out of what you make.

"You don't have a car right now, so you can walk from Gary's house with your mower. I'll also buy you a trimmer and a broom. Once you see a yard that needs to be mowed, go knock on the door and quote them a fair and reasonable price. Then give that yard the best mowing it's ever had.

"We'll have some signs made up that say 'Yards by Tony' with your phone number. You can put those in the yards when you are done. This is going to be a start, a way for you to make extra money."

"Yes, sir."

"You keep saving that 10 percent like we've talked about. You can add more, but never save less than 10 percent. Eventually you'll have enough to buy a nice used pickup truck. Then expand the area you mow. After that

Don't always talk about yourself.

you can buy a trailer and more equipment and hire some people to work for you. Are you getting this?"

"Yes." By now I had a picture in my mind of me driving my employees around in my truck, just like Gary does.

"Now, this is a simple plan, but that doesn't mean it's going to be easy. The real challenge is going to come down to your self-discipline.

"Most people don't have enough self-discipline to do what you've been doing. Most people, when they want something new, like a car, don't save. They rush out and buy it on credit. If you save and pay cash, you can negotiate a better deal. Plus you're not paying interest to someone else. When you borrow money, you become a slave to the lender.

"Let me know when you're ready to buy a truck. We'll find something that's been well maintained and cared for."

"Yes, sir." I was so excited by the idea that I couldn't think of anything else to say.

Finish what you start.

~18~

GOLD

Three days later, and just like Malcolm had promised, I pushed my lawnmower, trimmer, and broom out of Gary's garage and onto the street.

I stood at the end of the driveway, looked right and then left. *Guess it doesn't matter which way I go, the other side will be there tomorrow*, I thought. I turned right and headed up the street.

The owners of the first two houses I checked on were polite, but they told me no. The third house I stopped at really needed to have its yard mowed. It looked like it hadn't

Concentrate.

been mowed in weeks. I left my equipment on the street, walked up the driveway, and knocked on the door.

An elderly woman appeared at the glass door and opened it.

"Yes, sweetie?" she said to me.

"Ma'am, I was wondering if you would be interested in having me mow your yard?"

She sighed. "Well, I'd love to have it mowed. It sure does need it. But I just can't afford it right now. My husband used to mow it, but he passed away last month."

I looked at her and then the yard. I wasn't sure what to do. I spoke, almost without thinking. "I'll mow it for free." There was no way I was going to walk away from that house without helping that lady. This was my chance to help someone in need.

She looked at me. "I couldn't accept that."

"Ma'am, it would be my pleasure. I insist."

She smiled. "Thank you so much. Money's been so tight and I just didn't know how I was going to get the yard mowed. You are an answer to my prayers. Thank you."

I started the mower and went to work on the backyard. I was grateful that I had the chance to help someone else.

Dishonesty costs everything.

As I finished the front yard, a black Mercedes pulled up to the curb. The window rolled down and the driver motioned for me to come over.

"Yes, sir?" I asked as I leaned down to the window.

"I live down the street. I need my yard mowed. What do you charge?"

"Twenty-five bucks, including trimming."

"Kid, you got a deal. Just let me know when you're ready. I'll park my car in front of my house."

It didn't sound so bad being called "kid" that time. After all, he was going to be my first paying customer.

I knocked on the lady's door after I finished her yard.

"All done," I said proudly.

"Thank you so much. I wish there was some way that I could repay you."

"You're welcome. Please don't worry about repaying me. It's a privilege and an honor to be able to help you."

I headed to the house of the man who owned the Mercedes. I knocked on the door and let him know that I was going to start to mow.

"Just let me know when you are finished," the man said.

Motivate yourself.

I fired up the mower and began working. I was finished an hour later.

"Let's take a look," said the man when I knocked on his door again.

I had done the best job I could. The entire yard was cut to a uniform height and all the clippings had been neatly swept and bagged. The edges and the areas around the trees had been trimmed.

The man nodded in approval. "Good job, kid, good job." He reached in his pocket and handed me thirty bucks. "Thanks for going the extra mile. Here's a five-dollar tip."

I smiled and took the money, thanking him. "Sir, may I have permission to put a sign in the front yard?"

He agreed and I thanked him again. I pushed my mower around the corner. When I got out of sight of the man's house I stopped and pulled the money out of my pocket. *I can't believe how good it feels to hold this money in my hands — this thirty bucks might as well be a pound of gold. I didn't know that making money could feel this good.*

This was money I made myself, with my own business. I had listened to Malcolm's advice about owning a business and it made sense, but seeing those bills fanned out in my hand made it real.

Be real.

It was true. I owned my own business. I had made thirty dollars, and it only took an hour. I put the money back in my pocket and headed up the street, looking for the next yard to mow.

By the end of the summer, I built my business up to ten yards a week, and I was charging twenty-five dollars per yard. Following the plan that Malcolm had created for me, I had managed to save almost three thousand dollars. It was time to buy a used truck.

Malcolm and I browsed the newspaper ads. We found a five-year-old truck. It was spotless, just like Gary's and Malcolm's. The owner said he had bought it to help out while his daughter was in college. It had high miles but they were all highway miles, and he had every maintenance record. There was no doubt that this truck had been well cared for.

Two hours later, I became the owner of the truck. Malcolm and I went to the insurance agent where Malcolm helped me get insurance.

Back at Gary's house, I stood in the yard and looked at the truck shining in the sun. I couldn't believe it was really mine.

Seek understanding.

The following Saturday instead of Gary driving me to the lighthouse, I drove Gary. Gary told me how proud he was that I was able to buy my own truck.

Malcolm was waiting on us. As we started running, he asked, "So how's business?" It amazed me that Malcolm was asking me *and* Gary. We were both business owners. I couldn't help but smile.

Gary started. "It's going great ⁓ best it's ever been. In fact, I've had so much going on that I've had to refer some work to Lance. You know, the guy that quit on me. He's been sending me commissions."

"Really? That's great." Malcolm smiled. "That's one of the reasons I told you to help him be successful. If you hadn't done that, you would have lost money. Not only was it the right thing to do, but you are also making money. Never burn a bridge. You might have to cross it again and you never know where it will lead you."

I listened, but I couldn't believe what I was hearing. "Let me get this straight. Gary, are you saying that you told somebody to hire Lance and they did? And then Lance paid you?"

Gary and Malcolm laughed. Malcolm explained, "Yes, Tony, that's right. By sending that work to Lance, Gary

Become wise.

made sure the customer was going to have the work done by somebody Gary knew would do a good job. Plus, Lance paid Gary. And, someday, the shoe may be on the other foot. Lance may have too much work and send his overflow to Gary. Gary wouldn't be in this situation if he hadn't made the decision to help Lance."

I thought about that as we continued to run. I couldn't believe Malcolm was teaching me so many ways to make money. Sometimes it seemed like he could just pull money out of the air.

A few minutes later Malcolm asked me another question that would change my life. "Tony, have you ever thought about running a marathon?"

"No! I mean, that's about twenty-six miles, isn't it?"

"That's right, well, 26.2 to be exact."

"How could I run that far?"

"Well, you're already running nine around the lake. If you can run nine, you can run a marathon. You may have to slow down or even walk part of it, but you can do it. Trust me, you're already capable. I know it. And I know you could do it in under five hours."

I thought for a moment. *Why run that far?*

Use your talents.

It was like Malcolm was reading my mind. The next thing he said was, "Because people with self-esteem do esteemable things."

I got quiet. I wasn't sure about running that far, but once again I knew that if Malcolm recommended it, it was something that I could do. I started trying to figure out just how far 26.2 miles was. My math skills had improved since I started my own business, and it didn't take long for me to realize that 26.2 miles was almost three times around the lake.

Malcolm's voice interrupted my division. "There's a marathon next month in Chicago. Gary and I are going, and you're welcome to join us."

Gary chimed in, "Running a marathon is one of the coolest things you'll ever do. Dude, I can't tell you why, but when you finish it's like every good thing you've ever done rolled up into one."

Malcolm nodded. "You'll never forget your first marathon. I've done forty-one and I can still remember my first. Do you want to run the marathon with us?"

"Yes, I'll do it."

Malcolm smiled and continued the run in silence, appearing lost in his memories.

Everyone needs help.

 19

26.2 MILES

I tried really hard to focus in on my newest goal. I was running three days a week on my own. Until now, running was important, but I hadn't taken the individual runs seriously. On Monday I went to the mall and bought a running watch. Nothing too fancy, just something that would allow me to set a pace and stick to it, or even exceed it. I started timing my runs and writing the times down in my journal. By Thursday's run I had reduced my time by fifteen minutes. I was going to take whatever action necessary to finish the marathon in less than five hours.

Everyone suffers.

Three Thursdays later, Gary and Malcolm and I loaded up Malcolm's van and started the eight-hundred-mile trip from Oklahoma City to Chicago. Just like Malcolm's car, the van was used but immaculate. I had plenty of room to myself.

We talked the whole way to Chicago. The van had a TV and a great stereo, but most of the time they were off. We talked about making money, family, marathons, traveling, and religion. More than once Malcolm reminded Gary to follow the plan that they had created for his business to grow.

"It doesn't happen by accident, Gary. You won't just wake up one day with a multimillion-dollar business. You stick to the plan we made and watch your business grow."

I had to ask, "Gary, is it really your plan to have a multimillion-dollar business?"

"Yes. Malcolm and I have been working on that since I got released."

I couldn't believe Gary had set such a high goal for himself. Even more impressive, though, was the fact that Gary was on his way. I could see Gary's business growing and that he was on his way to having his home paid for. I had no doubt that Gary would make this happen.

Always take action.

"Tony, Gary isn't doing anything that you can't do. With the right knowledge and action, you can grow your business as well."

I thought for a second and said, "How big do I want to grow it?"

"How big do you want it to be?"

On Sunday, the day of the marathon, we were up at 5:00 A.M. The race started at 6:30. We left the hotel while it was still dark.

Malcolm followed the map he had printed out on his home computer and was laughing back and forth with Gary. I couldn't laugh. I was so nervous I felt like I was going to vomit. Malcolm parked in a public lot and we walked to the staging area where the race would start. Even this far away there were thousands of people in running gear, all headed in the same direction.

"Man, how many people are here?" I asked in disbelief. I had no idea there would be so many runners.

"About 40,000," Malcolm replied.

We made our way to the area where we waited for the run to start. We weren't close to the front. We would not be able to keep the pace set by the front-runners, and by

Don't run from challenges.

staying back we would not spend the first few miles avoiding faster runners.

"Don't you just love the excitement here?" Malcolm asked, smiling as he looked at all the people stretching, jumping, and even running in place — whatever they could do to try and calm their nerves.

I forced a smile and nodded. I wasn't sure what to do. The run hadn't even started yet and my heart was already pounding out of my chest. I looked at all the other people and suddenly felt like an outsider. They all looked so fit, so serious. I began to think there was no way I would be able to do this run.

Malcolm put his hand on my shoulder. "Don't let this psych you out. You can do this. I'll be right here with you. We'll do it together."

My fears disappeared. Now instead of being afraid, I was excited, looking forward to the challenge of running 26.2 miles with Malcolm and Gary.

Malcolm said, "Let's pray and ask God to help us with this marathon." It was a short prayer. When Malcolm prayed, he asked for strength, courage, and wisdom. He always ended with words of gratitude.

Off in the distance, at the head of the pack of runners,

Make a difference.

I heard an electronic beep signal the start of the run. A small cheer went up. The runners ahead of me started to move. The entire pack opened up and I ran to keep up with the people in front of me. I must have been a little too eager.

"Whoa! Easy, Tony. We've got a long way to run. Don't worry about keeping up with them. What we want to do, for at least the first few miles, is to run about an eight- or nine-minute pace. Slow down."

"You bet!" I was so jacked up about being in this run I yelled at Malcolm. I didn't mean to; it was just because I was so excited.

I slowed down and found a spot next to Malcolm. Gary was on the other side. I matched their pace and we went down the course.

There was a marker every mile. At the first mile marker, Malcolm looked at his watch. "Good. Right where we want to be." I looked at my watch, but in all the excitement I had forgotten to start the timer when the run began. I decided to just focus on keeping my legs moving.

By the third mile marker, I felt completely comfortable. Malcolm, Gary, and I were moving along at our usual pace. Except for the scenery and the 39,997 other people

Have faith.

with us, we might as well have been on Lake Hefner on any given Saturday.

At almost every intersection the cross street was blocked so that the runners wouldn't have to worry about oncoming traffic. There was usually a police officer directing traffic.

At each intersection, Malcolm got the officer's attention and said thank you.

After about the tenth time, I asked Malcolm why he was doing that. I'd never known anyone to thank police officers.

"There are two reasons. First, it's polite. Most of these officers are volunteering to be here. They're taking time out of their schedule so that we can run. I want to encourage them.

"Second, I admire what the police do. They put their lives on the line every day for the rest of us. That is worthy of my respect."

I looked at Malcolm, almost in disbelief. I had never heard anyone talk about the police in such good terms. I shook my head and thought, *Man, I've been living on the wrong side of the law for too long.*

The mile markers flew by. We stopped at a booth at

Give back.

mile seven to get a drink of water and then quickly got back into our rhythm.

When we passed mile marker nine, I realized that I was doing something that I had never done before. But there were plenty of things I had done in the past three months that were new. I was in new territory. I must have slowed my pace slightly, without even realizing it.

Malcolm noticed and said, "We just passed mile marker 9. Don't let this bother you. Gary and I are with you. We'll help you finish this and cross the finish line together. Just keep moving forward."

It worked. My pace increased.

By mile marker 11, I lost whatever fears I'd had at mile 9. My legs felt good and Malcolm and Gary were with me. I had a long way to go, and I knew that, but I was actually starting to believe that I would make it to the end.

At mile 13 Malcolm spoke up. "Halfway there. Just repeat what you've already done and we'll be finished."

"Yes, sir." I tried to focus on just moving. I didn't want to stop, slow down, or think about how far I had gone or how far I had to go. Just keep moving. But my legs started to hurt and I began to doubt if I could really make it.

"Man, I just don't know if I can do this," I told Malcolm.

Be loyal.

"You can. We'll stick together and make it."

We passed mile marker 14. The course was flat and straight. Several blocks ahead, in the middle of the course, we saw a lone runner having a difficult time. It was a girl and she stood out because the other runners were passing her on both sides. She ran a few feet and then stopped.

We jogged toward her and watched her almost fall. She stopped running, put her hands on her hips, and shook her head. Gary and I moved to the left side and began to pass her. I was already looking for the next mile marker.

I heard Malcolm's voice over my right shoulder. "Are you okay?" he asked the girl.

"Yes, I'm fine," she said sarcastically. "I just can't go on anymore. I put all this time into training for a marathon, and now I can't finish...." Her voice trailed off.

I stopped running and watched Malcolm talk to the stranger. I could see tears well up in her eyes.

"Is this your first marathon?" Malcolm asked.

"Yes." She reached up and wiped a tear from her cheek.

"Come with us. We'll finish this together. What's your name?"

"Heather," she answered. She seemed a little taken

Sympathy.

aback by the kindness she was being shown by a complete stranger.

"I'm Malcolm. That's Tony and Gary. This is Tony's first marathon, too."

I couldn't believe what I was hearing. "Malcolm, if we're going to finish this in under five hours, do you really think..."

Malcolm put up his left hand and stopped me. "Tony, we have the chance to help Heather finish her first marathon. Now we can go ahead and finish on our own, or we can help someone else finish their first marathon. Would you rather be *successful* or would you rather be *significant*?"

I knew there would be no discussion. Helping Heather was the right thing to do. I regretted saying anything to Malcolm. I had allowed my adrenaline to speak and not my brain.

"All right, let's finish this bad boy," Malcolm said with a smile. Heather took a breath and started running again. We joined in with her. We went slowly at first, allowing Heather to set the pace. After about half a mile, she started running faster.

We kept going, sometimes slow, sometimes fast, but

Take vitamins.

always going forward. At mile 17 we ate bananas and drank water.

"If we stay focused we can still make it in under five hours," Malcolm said as he took off.

At mile 20 I could tell the run hit Heather like a ton of bricks. She was struggling just to move, much less keep pace with us. She stopped and put her hands on her knees.

"My legs feel like they are on fire."

Malcolm said, "Come on, Heather, work through it."

Gary added, "You can do this."

"Don't stop now. We're almost done. We can finish this together, Heather," I said. "Just stick with me and we'll both be able to say we ran a full marathon. I'm right with you."

Heather walked, and then jogged a few, small steps. She kept that up for about a mile. I stayed with her.

"Guys, my legs have finally loosened up. I'm not as fresh as when I started, but I'm through the pain," she finally told us.

We kept moving toward the finish line. The mile markers passed by ⁓ 22, 23, 24.... I didn't take the time to think about how far we had gone, and I barely noticed the signs. They were just one more thing on the side of the road.

Miracles happen.

Mile marker 25 came and went. We followed the course around a corner and turned right. People were lining the street. Heather started to slow down.

I looked down the street. Just a few blocks away I saw a big banner overhead marking the finish line. Below it stood an electronic clock that displayed the time elapsed since the marathon began: 4:46. We still had time to make it in less than five hours.

I was suddenly overtaken by pain. I stopped running and started walking. Heather joined me. I could tell by the look on her face that she was in pain, too.

"Tony! Heather! Look at the finish line. Don't stop!" Malcolm yelled.

"Tony, keep going. We can still finish in under five hours!" I heard Gary say.

I heard everything, even people from the crowd cheering for us. The problem was that I couldn't get my legs to do what I needed. I was exhausted. There was no adrenaline left. I had been running for almost five hours and my fight was nearly gone.

I looked up at the finish line again. My mind focused like it never had before. The only thought I had was for me and Heather to cross that line together.

Share in other people's joy.

I kept going. It might have been quicker to walk, but I had been running all morning and right now that seemed like a more natural motion. Heather must have felt me speed up. I could see her plodding along on my right side.

"Heather, we're almost there. Whatever it takes, don't stop. Stay with me. We're going to finish this together."

I could hear people in the crowd cheer us on.

"You're almost finished!"

"You rock!"

"Keep your eyes on the finish line!"

By now I could almost reach out and touch the finish line. Heather was by my side. Malcolm and Gary were a few steps back. They wanted me and Heather to finish together.

Heather and I managed one more step. We were now almost underneath the banner. We took another step and were finally past the finish line. I looked up at the clock: 4:59:07 ~ less than a minute to spare.

I bent over and put my hands on my knees. I thought about what it meant to cross the finish line. What a difference forcing myself to run the last few miles had meant. Had I stopped just a few feet short of the finish line, there would be no sense of accomplishment. No joy.

Be social.

But I *had* finished. I had just run 26.2 miles and had helped Heather run her first marathon. This was an experience I would be proud of for the rest of my life. Malcolm's words went through my mind: "People with self-esteem do esteemable things."

I thought about all the things that had happened since I had met Malcolm. I was out of jail, had a new job, was a small business owner, and had finished a marathon. It was overwhelming. Tears streamed down my face.

Gary came up and patted me on the back. "Awesome. You made it in under five hours."

Heather came up and thanked me. "I couldn't have done it without you," she said, giving me a hug.

It felt great to know I helped her finish a marathon. She let go and disappeared into the arms of her family.

I walked over to Malcolm. Malcolm held his hand up and we high-fived. I told Malcolm, "Thanks for motivating me to do things I'd never even thought about."

With action great things will happen.

≈**20**≈

FEAR

Three weeks later when I met Malcolm for our Saturday morning run, I could tell that something was wrong. Malcolm didn't start off with his usual greeting or jokes and there was silence as we made our way around the lake.

After a few minutes I got up the nerve to ask Malcolm, "Is everything okay?"

Malcolm shook his head and I knew there was a problem. Malcolm wasn't talking and his pace wasn't as fast as it usually was.

Malcolm let a few moments pass. "I got some terrible

Significant people recognize significant actions.

news at work. We bought some accounting software, and it's not doing what it's supposed to do."

I could tell by his voice that it must have been a real problem. I wasn't sure what to do or say.

"All of our financial data was based on that software — my cash flow, inventory, everything — and none of it is right.

"Everything I relied on showed me I was making about fifty thousand dollars profit per month. But it turns out that instead of making fifty thousand dollars per month, the business was actually *losing* that much."

I almost stopped running. I could hardly believe anyone actually made fifty thousand dollars a month, and I sure couldn't imagine losing it.

Malcolm continued, "My inventory is way off. Everything is almost the exact opposite of what I thought. The long and short of it is that instead of having a business worth millions of dollars, the business is actually that far in debt."

I offered what I could. "Malcolm, I don't know what to say, but if I can do anything for you, all you have to do is ask."

Appreciate your life.

We kept jogging. Neither of us spoke and the silence amplified the seriousness of Malcolm's problem.

"That's not all," Malcolm said. "My company is also being sued. The law firm says that the way I contact new customers is illegal. It's a class action lawsuit, and it could wind up costing...." Malcolm took a deep breath before continuing, "...200 million dollars."

I watched Malcolm's face turn white. His pace slowed down. It looked like he had aged twenty years since last week.

"My lawyer says not to worry, that we can reach some understanding. But even if I win the lawsuit, this could wind up costing me everything. I could lose my business, my house, *everything*. One of these things is bad enough, but to have the two happen at the same time...."

By now we were on the north side of the lake heading east toward the lighthouse. Malcolm was struggling to find any reason to keep moving forward, and I slowed down to stay with him. I had never seen him so stressed.

"I just don't understand this. I've put everything into building my business. I've always tried to think of my employees and other people first. My employees all seem to be happy...." Malcolm's voice trailed off.

Creation, not competition.

"Malcolm, what are you going to do?" I asked.

It took a few moments. He looked at me, shrugged his shoulders, and said, "I don't know. I've never been in this situation before. I'm going to get some help from other people that have gone through this."

We trudged along, hampered by the weight on Malcolm's shoulders.

"I'm really scared."

Teach other people.

~21~

COURAGE

On Wednesday I called Malcolm. Gary and I had talked and we were both worried about him. Malcolm was usually so confident and knowledgeable. The fear I had seen in his eyes was shocking.

I called at ten in the morning. Malcolm answered the phone, but he still had sleep in his voice. I knew his routine was to wake up at five in the morning and I couldn't picture him sleeping until ten.

"Malcolm, it's Tony. I just wanted to check on you. Are you doing all right?"

Take action.

"Yeah, I'm fine."

"I was wondering if I could come run with you today. I know Wednesday is your usual day to run."

There was a long pause. "I don't know if I'm going to run today. I don't have the energy."

"Malcolm, you're always telling me how important exercise is. About how it makes you feel better. I will come run with you."

"Okay, Tony, meet me at my house at five."

I arrived at 4:45. I brought a book with me because Malcolm had taught me that if you have a book to read, you never have to wait. I was thumbing through the pages when he came out at 5:05.

Malcolm walked to my truck and I got out. I had never seen him unkempt before. It looked like he had slept in his shirt, it was so wrinkled. His hair, normally carefully groomed, had the impression from a pillow on the left side. It was the worst case of bed head I'd ever seen.

"Tony, I don't know if I can do this. I'm really tired."

"I need for you to run with me. If you want, we'll make it a short one. Let's go," I said.

Malcolm nodded.

I noticed that he didn't even look me in the eyes. We

Ask questions.

started running down the street. His pace was slow, even slower than the Saturday run at the lake. I had to slow down to avoid leaving him behind.

A few minutes into the run Malcolm said, "Thanks for running with me today. I know I need to exercise, but it's been hard for me to even get out of bed. I've been so depressed lately. It's unbelievable how everything in my life has just fallen apart.

"I was talking to my wife, Leslie. I told her we might lose everything. The one thing I don't want to lose is my family. Situations like this can tear a family apart and wind up in divorce court. We've recommitted ourselves to each other. We're going to stick together no matter what."

About five minutes into the run he actually laughed. It seemed like the exercise was already working its magic.

We plodded along through Malcolm's neighborhood. I wasn't sure what to say. I knew he was in real trouble. Seeing him like this, in such despair, so broken, shattered my heart.

Malcolm had given me a new life, hope, and a future. I wanted to do something for him, but I felt powerless. How could I ever repay him for what he had done for me?

Learn. Teach. Do.

What did I have to offer him — the owner of a multimillion-dollar business? I was just a few months out of jail.

We continued through the neighborhood. I didn't know how far he would want to go; I was just glad Malcolm was doing something. I let him set the pace and the route.

We made it back to his house thirty minutes later. We had run almost three miles. We stopped running when we reached my truck.

Malcolm told me to wait and he went inside his house. He came back with two bottles of water and handed one to me.

A light went on in my head. I realized that I could make a difference in his life. He had done so much for me, and I was excited I would have the chance to give something back. I decided I would run with Malcolm on the four days he normally ran and I would show up early in case he didn't feel like running. That would give me time to encourage him to go.

"Malcolm, you've given me so much and taught me so many new things. Just being with you has changed the way I think and look at life. One of the things that you have

Finish what you start.

taught me is to help other people out when they are in need. Right now, you need help.

"I want to help you. I will come see you every Tuesday, Wednesday, and Friday. Saturday we have our run at the lake. We will run together. I know that you're having a tough time with your business and that life seems to be crowding in on you. I'm going to make sure that you keep exercising."

Malcolm thought for a moment and said, "Thank you, Tony."

For six weeks, I kept my commitment. We ran every Tuesday, Wednesday, Thursday, and Saturday. Some days he wanted to run, some days he didn't.

Today it was a struggle just to get him out of the door. I showed up fifteen minutes early for the 5:00 P.M. run. I brought a book and read. I waited until 5:15. I put down the book and went and knocked on his door. I waited several minutes and knocked again.

Malcolm finally opened the front door. He looked as bad as I had ever seen him. He hadn't shaved, his hair was completely messed up, and his clothes looked like he had been wearing them for days. I tried not to notice.

Have integrity.

"Come on, Malcolm, let's go." I wanted to cry. I was shocked at how messy my mentor was.

Malcolm shook his head. "I'm not going today. Don't feel like it. Maybe next time." He stepped back and started to close the door. I fought the urge to grab the doorknob and stop him.

"Malcolm, I really want you to come with me today. I can tell you feel bad. The run will make you feel better."

He paused and looked at me. "Give me a minute. I need to go change."

As Malcolm left, I let out a sigh of relief. I wasn't sure what I would have done if he had said no to the run, but I did know that he needed to exercise. I would have done whatever it took to get him to go running.

Malcolm appeared in a moment, dressed in his running gear. Just the change from his rumpled clothes made him look better.

"Let's go," I said, gratified that he was coming.

"I don't know how far I can go."

"Just keep going. One step at a time. One foot in front of the other."

Malcolm was silent. That really bothered me. He was

Have values.

normally cheerful and jovial, but getting him to say any-thing was like pulling teeth.

We jogged slowly for a few blocks without any conver-sation at all. I finally asked, "How are you doing?"

He took a moment before he answered. "Things have gotten worse. I had to lay off a bunch of people, over half of my company. Plus, the bank has been calling me in two or three times a week. They're treating me like a little boy. I feel like I'm being called into the principal's office."

I couldn't imagine that things had gotten any worse for him.

We were going slowly, but at least we were going. I'd learned that getting Malcolm to talk was the hard part. Once he started talking, he would keep going.

He continued, "There are rumors everywhere. I don't know how all this got out, but I'm getting calls from friends and customers wondering what's happening with my business."

Malcolm paused. I knew he wasn't finished telling me what was going on.

"I got so depressed last week that I went to see a doctor. He diagnosed me with situational depression. He recom-

Be a mentor.

mended that I get on an anti-depressant, but I'm not going to take it.

"The problem is that I need to make changes in my life. Things feel like they are getting worse, but I have to keep taking action.

"I had to make some tough decisions. Three of my top sales people quit. They produced about half of the profit for the company. That's what caused the layoff.

"People have told me to bankrupt the company and close the business. I'm not going to do that. I'm not running from my responsibilities.

"I feel like I'm being tested. I don't understand why. I'm going to do whatever it takes to get out of this. I'm going to do what you did, Tony. I'm going to find a mentor, someone who can help teach me how to move past this."

I could feel Malcolm pick up the pace.

"I'm going to read and learn as much as I can. And I'm going to start going back to church. It's been a long time, but I know that will make a difference."

Listen well.

ᨪ22ᨀ

A GOD THING

Several weeks later when we met at the lighthouse at Lake Hefner, Malcolm's spirits seemed much better. He held his head high and he was whistling.

"Morning, gentlemen. Gary, how's your business? Dig any good holes lately?"

We were too stunned to speak. After months of Malcolm being so depressed, it was refreshing to see him so positive. Malcolm seemed like his old self.

"Yeah, Malcolm, I moved a bunch of dirt last week," Gary responded.

Don't take things personally.

"Good. Guys, I just want you to know how much I appreciate all your help these last few months. I felt like I was going through a desert with no markers.

"But I've started going to church again. It had been a long time, and I had forgotten how beautiful and peaceful church could be.

"It's really giving me a new sense of hope. I know my life's in God's hands. I might still lose my business and everything financially, but I have a new commitment to God. It's all going to work out.

"I've started reading a book called *The Purpose Driven Life*. It's helping me understand the type of actions I should take. You guys should read it."

For the first time in months, Malcolm was setting a fast pace. I could feel how much stronger and more confident he was this week.

"Do you two want to go to church with me and my family tomorrow?"

"Yeah, I'll go." I wasn't really sure I wanted to go, but it had obviously done wonders for Malcolm.

"No, thanks, Malcolm. I'm not ready to go," Gary replied.

Give away a book.

"No problem. Just remember that you're welcome to go if you change your mind."

We finished the run in a pace and with a joy we hadn't known in months.

On Sunday morning, I met Malcolm, Leslie, and their children at Malcolm's house. We loaded into the van and headed to church. Malcolm explained about his new church.

"I really like this church, Tony. The minister is dynamic. I can't wait for you to see and hear how great this guy is."

I wasn't really excited about going to church, but I knew all of the good things that it had done for Malcolm. And because it made him so happy, I was willing to go.

"Tony, what's really been good for me is the Sunday school class. The church is big. The Sunday school class is more intimate and has allowed me to meet people one on one. Those people have really helped me out. We'll get there in time for you to go to Sunday school. I'm not sure where your class meets, but we will find that out once we get there."

Malcolm parked the van and we went inside. I couldn't

Open doors for people.

believe how open and spacious the church was. I had gone to church a few times with my mom, but nothing had prepared me for how beautiful this one was. It was a sunny day and the sunlight illuminated the sanctuary.

Leslie took the girls and headed toward Sunday school. "Bye, honey. See you in class," she said to Malcolm, with the two kids in tow.

We found out where my Sunday school class would be held. Malcolm showed me where his family would be sitting during the service.

"Meet us here when class is over," he told me. I headed to the classroom.

There were several other people in the classroom. I took a deep breath and walked in. The other people came up to greet me. The last one was a girl.

"Hi, my name is Katie," she said as she put out her hand and shook mine.

After class I met Malcolm and his family in the sanctuary. I listened to the sermon and agreed with Malcolm. The preacher was engaging and inspiring.

"I feel like he's speaking right to me," I whispered to Malcolm.

After the service was over Malcolm introduced me to

Be a giver.

members of the church. Katie, the girl from Sunday school class, approached me and said the class was going out for lunch and asked if I would like to come along.

I glanced at Malcolm. "Sure, but I came with Malcolm. He's my ride home."

Katie smiled. "Don't worry. We'll get you home safe." It was the most beautiful smile I had ever seen.

"See you back at the house. Have fun, Tony," Malcolm said.

"Let's go," Katie said with a smile. We walked to the door and met up with the rest of the class.

Katie looked like she was in really good shape. She was wearing a dress and had a hard body. Her big brown eyes sparkled and she smiled a lot. When she smiled, I felt accepted and approved. I couldn't take my eyes off of her and I hoped she didn't think I was staring. I didn't know where we were going to eat, and I didn't care. I was just glad to be with her.

I'd never had a real girlfriend. I mean, there had been girls, but none I'd been serious about. And none of them had been as beautiful and friendly as Katie. She was so beautiful I had a hard time speaking to her.

We went to a Mexican place. The tables had real table-

Ask questions.

cloths — not paper like the places I usually went to. I ordered something with chicken. I remembered that Malcolm once told me that if you're ever in a restaurant and don't know what to eat, get chicken. Most places can't mess that up.

We talked and laughed while we waited for our food. I sure was glad I'd gone to church. The waitress brought us chips and salsa. I was so hungry I could have eaten the whole basket by myself, but I didn't want to look like a pig in front of Katie. We all had a lot of fun talking and laughing while we snacked on the chips.

Katie said the blessing when the food arrived. It was very thoughtful. She gave thanks for what we have and asked God to help us remember people who don't have as much as we do.

Katie laughed and looked at me. When our eyes met, my heart skipped a beat. I thought I didn't believe in love at first sight, but suddenly I found myself changing my mind.

I'm in love with Katie. She is beautiful, classy, and stylish. She listens to people. I love her looks, her voice, her laugh, and even the way she smells. Is this a God deal? Is this another miracle? I wondered.

Encourage others.

I smiled at Katie and thought, *She has my heart. She's perfect.*

The next Saturday on the lake run Malcolm was so excited that he could hardly be contained. After we exchanged the usual greetings, he said, "It's a miracle. You won't believe what happened to me this week."

Gary and I both asked what was going on.

"I've been praying about this for weeks. So has my Sunday school class.

"I kept wondering how I was going to get out of this financial mess. Then I realized I have one asset ⁓ my building. I decided to sell the building my company is in and move to a smaller place.

"It took me a long time to make the decision. I personally designed the building. I drew out the plans and made sure that it was as comfortable as possible for the employees. They had a great kitchen, beautiful bathrooms, and natural light. It really took a lot for me to decide to sell that place.

"But I had to. With the money left over after I pay off the mortgage, I can pay down most of the debt the company owes.

Listen well.

"What is really miraculous is that the day after I decided to sell the place, one of my former employees walked into my office out of the blue. Her name is Stacy. She asked me if I would be interested in selling. The company she works for now is expanding and she told them she knew of a great building. We'll go to closing soon and I'll have a check in my hand just twenty-eight days after I decided to sell it."

Malcolm shook his head in amazement and laughed.

"Sweet," I said — that was all I could think to say. I wish I knew more fancy words, but that was as good as I could do. I was relieved that my friend and mentor was feeling so good.

"To make things even better, remember the lawsuit that was filed against the company?"

"How could I forget you talking about $200 million dollars?" I asked.

"Well, I talked to my attorney and he told me the other lawyer agreed that the lawsuit was frivolous. We settled the lawsuit for almost nothing. It's over."

"Awesome. Malcolm, I'm so happy for you."

Move someone for free.

⇜23⇝

THE KID

Malcolm definitely succeeded in teaching me the importance of routine. For the last three years, I've followed the routine Malcolm helped me set up. I've done the same thing at the same time every day. Malcolm was right about the importance of routine. I've followed the plan we created and the results are amazing. My business has grown to the point that I no longer work for Gary. With his blessing, I have been working for myself full-time for the last two years. I employ six people.

Finish what you start.

My reading has really taken off. I read a lot. I try to read a book a week.

Best of all, I married Katie, the girl I met in church, and we have been married for a year and a half. Our first child is due in six months.

Gary's business is growing too. He now has thirty employees. Malcolm's business has recovered from its challenges and is doing better than ever.

So many amazing things have happened to me, but the most amazing is scheduled to take place today. I never dreamed this could happen.

Gary and Malcolm and I are at the Oklahoma state capitol. My wife is here as well. Last week Malcolm told me there was someone who wanted to meet me ~ someone important.

"Who's that?" I asked. I had no idea who would want to meet with me.

Malcolm smiled. "The governor." He paused to let that sink in. "He's heard about all that you've done in the last three years and he has something to give you."

"Me? The governor wants to give *me* something? What would he want to give me?" I couldn't believe the

Pick up trash.

governor would even know about me, much less have something for me.

Malcolm's smile got bigger. "A pardon. He's going to sign paperwork and you won't be a convicted felon anymore."

Now we are at the capitol, waiting to get my felony removed. We are outside the governor's office, near a receptionist sitting at her desk. Behind her is a frosted glass door. When the door opens, it's the governor.

"Hello, Malcolm," he says and the two shake hands.

"Good afternoon, Mr. Governor."

"Sir, I'd like for you to meet two of my friends. This is Gary, and this gentleman is the one that I have been telling you about. His name is Tony, and this lovely young lady is his wife, Katie."

Katie and I shake hands with the governor. I feel like I'm about to pass out.

The governor motions us back into his office, where he sits down at his very official-looking desk. It's actually the biggest desk I've ever seen.

I stand in front of the desk. The governor clears his throat, opens a folder, and pulls out a sheet of paper. I see

Be cheerful.

my name at the top but I can't see anything else on the page.

"The reason that we are here today is because of you, Tony," says the governor. "Malcolm has told me of all the things that you have been able to accomplish in the last three years."

He looks me in the eyes. "Tony, what you've done is a miracle. You have stayed out of trouble and now you own a successful business and employ other people. I know that you are a changed man. I am proud to put my signature on this document that pardons your prior felony conviction."

The governor uncaps his pen and signs the document. He has two other copies and signs both of those, handing one to me. He then stands up and shakes my hand. A camera clicks over my shoulder. I hadn't seen anyone with a camera when I came in.

My mind is a blur. I think over the last four years and how my whole life had changed because Malcolm took the time to mentor me. I fight to keep tears from falling.

Katie, however, doesn't even try to hide her tears. She stands behind me, beaming with pride and crying with joy.

Never again would I have to look anyone in the eye and say I'm a convicted felon. Part of me wants to go back to

Write a book.

the stores and restaurants that wouldn't hire me because I was a felon and wave the paper around, but I know better.

"Thank you, Mr. Governor." I am not sure what else to call him. I know it's not Your Highness.

"No, Tony. Thank you. It was my pleasure to review your life."

We make our way back to the hallway. Katie takes the paperwork from me and begins to read it. She throws her arms around my neck and starts weeping. "I'm so proud of you."

Gary shakes my hand, and I tell him, "Gary, thank you so much for all the help you've given me."

"My pleasure."

I look over to Malcolm. "Thank you so much for what you've done for me. You've taught me so much. Without you, I would have nothing."

Malcolm stops me. "Tony, thank you. Without you, I never would have gotten through the desert I was in. You helped me to keep running. You saved my life. I just want you to know, as I watched the governor give you a pardon, I don't know if I've ever felt more proud. I doubt I could be any prouder if one of my own daughters had just received her Ph.D."

Be kind.

Malcolm reaches out his hand to shake mine and for the first time, I feel like Malcolm and I are equals. He has taught me how to live a full life, and I helped him rebuild his.

"Time for me to go to group at the county jail. It's Tuesday. Tonight's my night. It's been rewarding for me to be able to give something back," I announced. "Plus, Jeff, the guy that was with me the night I was arrested for stealing beer, is in jail. I'm giving him a copy of *The Greatest Miracle in the World* tonight."

Save 10 percent.

www.MentorHope.com

FIND A MENTOR

You may now be wondering how *you* can find a mentor. Like everything in life, it will require taking action. You probably won't find someone who has success in all areas, but you can find people with success in different areas. Most successful people want to share their stories and help because they owe their success to people who helped them.

Where you look for a mentor depends on the type of mentor you want. Make sure the mentor has success and knowledge in the area in which you are seeking help. You wouldn't ask a bricklayer for advice on diamonds or a jeweler for advice on laying bricks. For a spiritual mentor, look in your church or local place of worship. For a financial mentor, look in the business section of your local newspaper.

You can also ask your friends and family. Most people have a much larger network of resources available than they realize. You'll be surprised what doors the contacts you already have can open.

Don't expect your mentor to be flawless. All people have strengths and weaknesses in different areas. You can even look at your mentor's weakness as an opportunity because you may be able to help your mentor grow in a weak area. Regardless of how successful a person is, he or she can always learn and become better at things. Likewise, regardless of where you are coming from or what you need to learn, there are some areas where you can teach others, including your mentor.

It's important that your mentor has time available to spend with you. Many people want to help, but their schedules may be so busy that they are not able to give the time necessary. Make sure your mentor is able to keep up with the time commitment.

Once you find someone you would like to seek advice

from, send him or her a brief note introducing yourself and asking for a mentoring relationship. Be sure to explain that you're not expecting a job, you just want advice. Successful people receive many requests — often from people who want the person to hire them even when there is no position available.

You're more likely to have success if you ask for a small amount of time. If the person is not able to help you, politely ask if they know someone else who might be able to help you.

It's important that there be good chemistry between you and your mentor. Your first meeting should be about fifteen minutes to see if you will get along. You don't want to go to meetings that are awkward or uncomfortable. You will learn more from someone you get along with than from someone you don't.

Every mentor has a different style. Make sure that whomever you select has a style and temperament that works well for you. Your mentor should believe in you and what you can accomplish together. If your mentor does not believe in your potential, the relationship will not grow.

Be sure to ask if your mentor is receiving any mentoring. It is important that anyone you seek help from realizes their shortcomings and is willing to take the time to overcome them. A good mentor understands that no one really stops learning. Anyone who stops learning stagnates.

Be prepared and enthusiastic. If you arrive at your meetings and it's obvious that you are there to learn, your mentor will be more willing to share his or her knowledge. The last thing a busy person wants is to feel like he or she is wasting time. Also, mentoring is a two-way street. A good mentor knows that someone who takes the relationship seriously will be a more valuable contribution.

Be patient and focused. Once you find a mentor, the results probably won't happen immediately. Listen to what your mentor says and put it into action. If you consistently apply the principles taught to you, over time you will see results.

BE A MENTOR

Mentoring takes time. Give careful thought to the time commitment you're willing to make. You must first decide which type of mentoring you will be offering, and your time constraints may help you with that decision.

There are three types of mentoring to choose from: personal mentoring, advisor/student mentoring, and indirect mentoring. The type of mentoring that was expressed between Malcolm and Tony is personal mentoring. This is when the mentor allows the student into his life and into his home. This is very powerful because it allows the mentor to show a real-life, living example for the student to model.

The second method is advisor/student mentoring. This is when the mentor and the student schedule a time every week to meet and go over material relating to the student's life. This method, if executed correctly, can be very powerful as well. To find out the most effective way to get the most out of the scheduled time, **visit www.mentorhope.com** and download the free mentor sheet.

The last method is indirect mentoring. This happens when the mentor recommends books, audios, or any further form of education to the student. The mentor does not directly advise the student; however, the mentor guides the student down a directed path that will impact the student's life. This is great for people who can't find the time to give in a more traditional mentoring relationship. This method also allows you to mentor many different people at once.

Next, you will need to find the right person to mentor. You probably already receive requests for your time. Agree to meet with a few of these people and let them tell you their situation. Tell them about how you have been able to achieve your success.

You may receive inquiries from people you work with or from people in organizations you belong to. When someone asks you about mentoring, agree to spend a few moments of your time.

Another way to find someone to mentor is to volunteer. Many groups have opportunities for people to donate their time and talents. If you take advantage of this, you will come in contact with numerous people who can benefit from your experience, skill, and expertise.

Mentoring is a great way to learn. You may meet someone who has a very different background than you. You will see things from a different perspective and grow from this. Even if you mentor someone from an environment similar to yours, he or she will challenge your knowledge in some areas. You will definitely grow as a result of mentoring.

C

THE LIST

Following is "The List." Please feel free to distribute this list by going to www.mentorhope.com and downloading a printed copy.

1. Finish what you start.
2. Have integrity.
3. Have values.
4. Be a mentor.
5. Stay committed.
6. Listen well.

7. Don't take things personally.
8. Give away a book.
9. Open doors for people.
10. Help others.
11. Ask questions.
12. Encourage others.
13. Move someone for free.
14. Finish what you start.
15. Pick up trash.
16. Be cheerful.
17. Write a book.
18. Be kind.
19. Save 10 percent.
20. Visit someone in the hospital.
21. Visit someone in treatment.
22. Believe in yourself.
23. Have a dream list.
24. Use a to-do list.
25. Don't worry.
26. Visit someone in jail.
27. Ideas. Action. Commitment.
28. Visit someone in a homeless shelter.
29. Buy someone dinner.

30. Exercise.
31. Take vitamins.
32. Finish what you start.
33. Winners take action.
34. Share hope.
35. Dream big.
36. Winners plan.
37. Call a friend.
38. Planners win.
39. Learn from other people.
40. Do good.
41. Use good manners.
42. Call a relative.
43. Have fun.
44. Become a champion.
45. Repay favors.
46. Don't assume anything.
47. Always be on time.
48. Go to a seminar.
49. Take a walk.
50. Go to the park.
51. Finish strong.
52. Read.

53. Sharing is caring.

54. Don't blame others.

55. Focus.

56. Exercise your mind.

57. Be slow to anger.

58. Be honest.

59. Give freely.

60. Creation, not competition.

61. Do important things first.

62. Carry a book with you.

63. Always do your best.

64. Develop routine.

65. Drink water.

66. Accept responsibility.

67. Stick to your plan.

68. Invite someone to church.

69. Enjoy church.

70. Be a greeter at church.

71. Run four days a week.

72. Reconciliation, not retaliation.

73. Be a person of value.

74. Value people.

75. Be loyal.

76. Say what you mean.
77. Save 10 percent.
78. Believe in others.
79. Impact the lives of others.
80. Mean what you say.
81. Read more.
82. Be polite.
83. Accept challenges.
84. Defeat challenges
85. Get a mentor.
86. Be a friend.
87. Keep your promises.
88. Be kind.
89. Go the extra mile.
90. Be frugal.
91. Thank people.
92. Use positive words.
93. Remember your victories.
94. What gets measured gets improved.
95. Stick to your plan.
96. Enjoy new things.
97. Save 10 percent.
98. Share good news.

99. Encourage others.
100. Avoid self-doubt.
101. Play by the rules.
102. Use kind words.
103. Don't always talk about yourself.
104. Finish what you start.
105. Concentrate.
106. Dishonesty costs everything.
107. Motivate yourself.
108. Be real.
109. Seek understanding.
110. Become wise.
111. Use your talents.
112. Everyone needs help.
113. Everyone suffers.
114. Always take action.
115. Don't run from challenges.
116. Make a difference.
117. Have faith.
118. Give back.
119. Be loyal.
120. Sympathy.
121. Take vitamins.

122. Miracles happen.

123. Share in other people's joy.

124. Be social.

125. With action great things will happen.

126. Significant people recognize significant actions.

127. Appreciate your life.

128. Creation, not competition.

129. Teach other people.

130. Take action.

131. Ask questions.

132. Learn. Teach. Do.

133. Do Yoga.

134. Yoga is cool.

135. Be a giver.

Remember, you can get a copy of this list at our website: www.mentorhope.com

READ!

For those who are interested in learning more about the ideas presented in this book, we recommend the following books.

- *Greatest Miracle in the World* by Og Mandino
- *How to Win Friends and Influence People* by Dale Carnegie
- *Think and Grow Rich* by Napolean Hill
- *The Purpose Driven Life* by Rick Warren
- *Unlimited Power* by Anthony Robbins
- *E-Myth Revisited* by Michael E. Gerber

- *7 Habits of Highly Effective People* by Stephen Covey
- *Richest Man in Babylon* by George S. Clason
- *One Minute Manager* by Ken Blanchard
- *Influence: Science and Practice* by Robert B. Cialdini
- *The Dream Giver* by Bruce Wilkinson
- *Financial Peace* by Dave Ramsey
- *See You at the Top* by Zig Ziglar
- *The Road Less Traveled* by M. Scott Peck
- *The Four Agreements* by Don Miguel Ruiz
- *In My Own Words* by Mother Teresa
- *No Greater Love* by Mother Teresa
- *A Simple Path* by Mother Teresa
- *First Things First* by Stephen R. Covey, A. Roger Merrill, and Rebecca R. Merrill
- *Copy This!* by Paul Orfalea and Ann Marsh
- *Built to Last* by Jim Collins and Jerry I. Porras
- *The Spell Binder's Gift* by Og Mandino
- *Key to Yourself* by Venice Bloodworth
- *Sam Walton: Made in America* by Sam Walton and John Huey
- *You and Your Network* by Fred Smith
- *Wake Up and Live* by Dorothea Brande

- *How to Read a Book* by Mortimer J. Adler
  and Charles Van Doren
- *Coming Out of the Ice* by Victor Herman
- *The Bible*
- *The Lessons of History* by Will Durant and Ariel Durant
- *Developing the Leader within You* by John C. Maxwell
- *Developing the Leaders around You* by John C. Maxwell
- *Guerrilla Marketing* by Jay Conrad Levinson
- *Principle Centered Leadership* by Stephen R. Covey
- *Tuesdays with Morrie* by Mitch Albom
- *The 7 Habits of Highly Effective Families* by Stephen R. Covey
  and Sandra Merrill Covey
- *The Millionaire Next Door* by Thomas J. Stanley
  and William D. Danko
- *The Wealthy Barber* by David Chilton
- *Men Are from Mars, Women Are from Venus* by John Gray
- *The Rainmaker* by John Grisham
- *Out of the Crisis* by W. Edwards Deming
- *Who Moved My Cheese?* by Spencer Johnson
  and Kenneth H. Blanchard
- *The Thinker's Way* by John Chaffee
- *The Selling Bible* by John F. Lawhon
- *Don't Fire Them, Fire Them Up* by Frank Pacetta

- *The Firm* by John Grisham
- *The Chamber* by John Grisham
- *Billy Bathgate* by E. L. Doctorow
- *The Ragamuffin Gospel* by Brennan Manning
- *A New Pair of Glasses* by Chuck C.
- *The Great Gatsby* by F. Scott Fitzgerald
- *The Autobiography of Benjamin Franklin* by
  Benjamin Franklin
- *When Life is a Barbed Wire Fence* by Greg Winston
- *God Owns My Business* by Stanley Tam
- *Jack: Straight from the Gut* by Jack Welch
  and John A. Byrne
- *The McKinsey Way* by Ethan M. Rasiel
- *Message in a Bottle* by Nicholas Sparks
- *Be Happy You Are Loved* by Robert H. Schuller
- *A Tale of Three Kings* by Gene Edwards
- *In the Heart of the World* by Mother Teresa
- *An Encounter with a Prophet* by Clyde A. Lewis
- *Small Miracles* by Yitta Halberstam
- *The Christmas Box* by Richard Paul Evans
- *Living Faith* by Jimmy Carter
- *The Celestine Prophecy* by James Redfield
- *The Deming Management Method* by Mary Walton

- *Rich Dad, Poor Dad* by Robert T. Kiyosaki
  and Sharon L. Lechter
- *The Performance Edge* by Robert K. Cooper
- *Corporate Lifecycles* by Ichak Adizes
- *How to Make Luck* by Marc Myers
- *The Change* by Robert Grupe
- *Trump: Surviving at the Top* by Donald J. Trump
- *A Passion to Win* by Sumner Redstone and Peter Knobler
- *The Millionaire Mind* by Thomas J. Stanley
- *Pushing the Envelope* by Harvey Mackay
- *The CEO Chronicles* by Glenn Rifkin and Douglas Matthews
- *Business Dad* by Tom Hirschfeld and Julie Hirschfeld
- *Prescription for Success* by Anne Morgan
- *Making a Habit of Success* by Mack R. Douglas
- *Business at the Speed of Thought* by Bill Gates
- *Zig Ziglar's Secrets of Closing the Sale* by Zig Ziglar
- *Prospecting Your Way to Sales Success* by Bill Good
- *Leap of Strength* by Walt Sutton
- *How to Have Power and Confidence in Dealing with People*
  by Les Giblin
- *The Keys to Empowerment* by Ken Blanchard, John P. Carlos,
  and Alan Randolph

- *Leadership by the Book* by Ken Blanchard, Bill Hybels, and Phil Hodges
- *Whale Done!* by Ken Blanchard, Thad Lacinak, Chuck Tompkins, and Jim Ballard
- *Bill Gates Speaks* by Janet Lowe
- *Living the 7 Habits* by Stephen R. Covey
- *On Becoming Baby Wise* by Gary Ezzo and Robert Bucknam
- *Seabiscuit* by Laura Hillenbrand
- *University of Success* by Og Mandino
- *God is Not in the Thesaurus* by Bo Don Cox
- *I Dare You!* by William H. Danforth
- *Turning Hurts Into Halos* by Robert H. Schuller
- *The One Minute Father* by Spencer Johnson
- *Hope from My Heart* by Rich DeVos
- *More Than Enough* by Dave Ramsey
- *Getting to Yes* by Roger Fisher and William Ury
- *It's Not about the Bike* by Lance Armstrong and Sally Jenkins
- *Kiss Theory Good Bye* by Bob Prosen
- *Tough Times Never Last, but Tough People Do!* by Robert H. Schuller
- *101 Reasons to Own the World's Greatest Investment* by Robert P. Miles

- *More Than a Pink Cadillac* by Jim Underwood
- *The Secrets Men Keep* by Stephen Arterburn
- *The Five Major Pieces to the Life Puzzle* by Jim Rohn
- *Gung Ho!* by Ken Blanchard and Sheldon Bowles
- *George Burns: In His Own Words* by Herb Fagen
  and George Burns
- *City Kid* by Mary MacCracken
- *Tex* by S.E. Hinton
- *An Uphill Climb* by Dave Sargent
- *The 3 Keys to Empowerment* by Kenneth Blanchard,
  John Carlos, and Alan Randolph
- *Freedom from Fear: Overcoming Worry and Anxiety* by
  Neil T. Anderson and Rich Miller
- *Vernon Can Read!* by Vernon E. Jordan, Jr.
  and Annette Gordon-Reed
- *Big Bucks!* by Kenneth Blanchard and Sheldon Bowles
- *When God Winks at You* by Squire Rushnell
- *The Prayer of Jabez* by Bruce Wilkinson
- *Grinding It Out: The Making of McDonald's* by Ray Kroc
  and Robert Anderson

THE AUTHORS

Tom Pace is the founder and CEO of PaceButler Corporation (www.pacebutler.com), which he launched in 1987. Since then he has grown PaceButler into a multimillion-dollar company with a national and international presence. Tom is happily married with two wonderful daughters. He enjoys reading, running, and skiing, as well as mentoring numerous individuals from diverse backgrounds. Tom is also passionate about expanding his reading and mentoring program through MentorHope, LLC, an organization started by his commitment to make the world a better place. To learn more, visit www.mentorhope.com. To learn more about Mr. Pace, visit his company website, www.pacebutler.com.

Walter Jenkins is the proud father of Katie Jenkins. Before beginning his career as a writer and speaker, he was an attorney and sports agent. He is a former managing editor of the Oklahoma City University School of Law *Law Review*, and he has edited and published articles on numerous subjects. In his spare time he enjoys studying tae kwon do, scuba diving, riding his bike, and training his German shepherd, Jake the wonder dog. Visit his website at www.walterbjenkins.com.

Learn. Teach. Do.

MENTOR·HOPE

Learn MORE about MENTORING

Visit our website to tell us your story, get help, or to learn more about starting a mentorship.

www.mentorhope.com

- Get links to resources
- Get more info & material
- Get helpful advice
- Connect with others
- Give us feedback
- Get inspired

The *Mentor: The Kid and the CEO* book or audiobook CD is a perfect tool for mentoring programs within correctional and rehabilitation institutions, community programs and organizations, faith communities, business, & education. These products are available in large quantities at special discounts for qualifying organizations. Please call 1-405-752-0940 to distribute these today.

NEW!

Audiobook CD!

Sometimes, reading is difficult... get started with our new audio CD. Available in bulk.

$19.97 182 minutes

ISBN: 978-0-9793962-9-8

Visit our site for info.